Thieves Like Us

THIEVES LIKE US

A Novel

By

EDWARD ANDERSON

FOREWORD BY JOHN H. TIMMERMAN

UNIVERSITY OF OKLAHOMA PRESS
NORMAN AND LONDON

Also by EDWARD ANDERSON

Hungry Men (1935)

Cataloging-in-Publication Information
Anderson, Edward, 1905–1969.
    Thieves like us : a novel / by Edward Anderson.
        p. cm.
    ISBN 0-8061-2503-9 (alk. paper)
    I. Title.
PS3501.N218T45   1993   92-29959
813'.52—dc20   CIP

The paper in this book meets the guidelines for permanence and durability of the Committee on Production Guidelines for Book Longevity of the Council on Library Resources, Inc. ∞

First published in 1937 by Frederick A. Stokes Company, New York. Published in 1993 by the University of Oklahoma Press, Norman, Publishing Division of the University. Foreword, by John H. Timmerman, copyright © 1993 by the University of Oklahoma Press. All rights reserved. Manufactured in the U.S.A. First printing of the University of Oklahoma Press edition.

1   2   3   4   5   6   7   8   9   10

To

MY COUSIN AND MY WIFE

BECAUSE THERE I WAS WITH AN EMPTY GUN
AND YOU, ROY, SUPPLIED THE AMMUNITION
AND YOU, ANNE, DIRECTED MY AIM

"Men do not despise a thief, if he steal to satisfy his soul when he is hungry; but if he be found, he shall restore sevenfold; he shall give all the substance of his house."

—*Proverbs of Solomon.*

FOREWORD

By John H. Timmerman

Those many myths that inhabit the Great Plains, spawned like restless spirits by the reluctant soil and the people who toil upon it, also infiltrate every nook and cranny of its literature. Each literary genre seems uniquely marked by the nature of the plains. The drama of the western, the teasing lure of the adventure yarn, the dream of the quest, the lineaments of a people's life in the regional tale—all these seem to mingle together in land and literature alike.

Edward Anderson, born in Texas in 1905 and having grown up there and in Oklahoma, pursued a writing career that ranged from journalism to pulp fiction. He rode the rails as a hobo through the depression years, appropriated those stories also, and in the strange alchemy of his literary craft, transformed all of his experience into something hauntingly unique. In addition to a stream of lesser work, Anderson published just two novels—*Hungry*

Men in 1935, which won a *Story* magazine prize, and the memorable *Thieves Like Us* in 1937—after which, in one of those anomalies of literary history, he wrote little but journalism until his death in 1969.

Anderson seemed to feel the spirit of the Great Plains in his very bones, and it affects his craft. *Thieves Like Us* is shot through with a sense of dislocation, of melancholy drifting, of urgent, even desperate, lives. But it is also shot through with a kind of desperado action that provides a gripping narrative adventure.

One is tempted, thereby, to label the novel "hard-bitten realism." If it is, then Anderson has bitten carefully, for he is careful not to let his characters fall into the stereotypes so often associated with the label. While he avoids sentimentality like a virus, the work is not devoid of sentiment. This gang of thieves—these Great Plains toughs—are, finally, people whose lives are twisted by fate but who claw their way in its very grip—not out of it—by looking for love, loyalty, and a brighter hope. While the brighter hope remains elusive as myth itself, love and loyalty penetrate the lives of these people with a reality and an immediacy that defy nearly everything fate tosses their way.

Anderson crafts a credible and moving story here, yet his reputation in American letters has been shifting and ephemeral. Initial reviews, including a laudatory one by Louis L'Amour, were favorable but few. Some, like Mark Van Doren, who saw the novel simply as a story about "gangsters of the plains," considered the work as an exercise in regionalism or merely a genre type. Nonetheless, the novel went through one reissue by Arbor House in 1986.

Why does the novel merit a reissue now? Apart from its regional interest, what enduring qualities mark this story of a trio of bank-busting thieves? Why does it deserve sustained and deliberate attention? There are three such qualities, and they are indeed meritorious ones that rank this novel as an enduring work of artistic merit.

First among them is the carefully honed and powerful style of the novel. In prose as lean and spare as a sharecropper's children, Anderson's work develops a compelling urgency. The one-time journalist brings to his story a reporter's eye, gifted at seizing life at a glance. We see sharply and vividly through this writer's glance: "The porch planks creaked and gave under Bowie's steps and then he knocked on the door. Under the half-raised blind he could see the trousered legs of men seated at a card table." From the initial lines—"like a saliva-wettened finger scorching across a hot iron, Bowie's insides spitted"—through dialogue as crisp and clean as flame, Anderson renders a taut, tough drama. If he brings the reporter's eye to the tale, however, it is an eye softened by imagery as fluid as tears: "the Jew's harp twanging of the grasshoppers"; "her eyes were the color of powdered burnt sugar"; "the front door of the Gusherton house parted and there was the smell of cold bacon and raw onion and then in the crack of light was Lula's watercolor face."

The stylistic energy surrounds a memorable cast of characters, for the second trait of greatness in this slim novel is Anderson's evocation of the lives of his characters. Typically he suggests more than he tells. The characters expand in significance even as the plot propels them resolutely toward their inevitable deaths. They live on the edge of risk, precariously, without time or energy for sustained reflection on the lives they live. Yet, they provide moment

after moment of insight that accumulates power-
fully.

The central cast, and an oddball bunch it is,
consists of only four.

T. W. Masefield, a.k.a. T-Dub, robbed his first
bank when he was a kid, cutting through the window bars on the day after Christmas and stealing
fourteen dollars in pennies in order to buy a bicycle. By the end of the novel he has made his thirty-
first bank heist, opening accounts across Texas and
Oklahoma with a .45 caliber deposit. Through it
all, he longs for life in a simple shack up in the
Kentucky hills.

Elmo Mobley, a.k.a. Three-Toed, a.k.a. Chicamaw, longs to raise some money for his folks—
"them folks of mine haven't got a pot or a window to
throw it out and I got to get them some money"—
but his compulsion to drink and gamble never
seems to leave him enough to send. Chicamaw is a
leech upon life, a no-good who tests his friends'
loyalties to the limit, but whose one enduring virtue
is itself loyalty. Tell Chicamaw you want to rob a
bank on the fifteenth and he'll be there. Probably
stone drunk, but he'll be there.

And, most importantly as the narrative voice of the novel, the bank-robbing trio is rounded out by Bowie Bowers. Bowie longs for a $5,000 stake so that he can quit thieving, but even when the stake passes $20,000, he can't quite break free. He is addicted to thieving. But, like Chicamaw, Bowie would call it loyalty instead.

And Bowie's loyalty is unsurpassed for the fourth major character, the irrepressible, oddly virtuous, if unethical, woman Keechie. She is a young beauty, despite her plank-thin body, and it is little wonder that Bowie falls in love with her. Keechie is insistent, however, upon all his love, and she is tough-minded enough to try to wean Bowie from his addiction, even to continue loving him when his loyalties clash like flaring comets in his brain.

It is a memorable cast of characters, supported by a host of lesser lives that pass tellingly through the pages and that linger long in the reader's mind. Out of the lowest of lives, an enduring humanity resonates, takes form, gropes toward meaning, and struggles against the bewilderment of place and circumstance.

The searching nature of the characters, their undercurrent of bewildered discontent, shapes the third major artistic quality of the novel, the thematic significance of which is foreshadowed by the title, *Thieves Like Us*. For thieves are not simply bank robbers: the thieves are all around us and within us. Although the social commentary is not overplayed in the novel, it always lurks there, a modulating rhythm sustaining the actions and reactions of the characters.

The theme develops subtly. As the novel is a retreat into a time past, it also uncovers layers of life, and a psychology of thievery. "Them politicians," T-Dub asserts, "are thieves just like us. Only they got more sense and use their damned tongues instead of a gun." Later, T-Dub reflects, "I should have made a lawyer or run a store or run for office and robbed people with my brain instead of a gun." Therein lies an odd vulnerability in the characters. They know they are part of a larger game. But they are poor players in it. The game plays them and they're bound to lose. "There are more no-good people in this world than there are good ones," observes Keechie, who is not particularly bad and certainly not evil in this world. In fact, recognizing their own thievery for what it is, the robbers also adopt a strange code of morality. It isn't just that the banks are insured, and the losses covered by "them billionaires in New York," as T-Dub observes, but it extends to a moral principle of thievery: "No sir, I've never robbed anybody in my life that couldn't afford to lose it. . . . You couldn't hire me to rob a filling station or hamburger joint."

In discourse with a wonderfully corrupt lawyer, whose corruption allows him to extend goodness to the thieves, Bowie observes, "I guess a man has to make a living." The lawyer responds, "In this system he is forced to be a criminal."

Thieves like us are all around us. Some are more flagrant than others; some more surreptitious and socially acceptable. The latter seldom get caught. The former are caught from the start, before the guns start blazing. Given that premise in Anderson's novel, how does one survive? In this curious little morality play, what moral end can one adopt?

One survives through loyalty, surely. For this detective-adventure regional western is also a story about love and loyalty. This is most apparent in the relationship between Bowie and his "Little Soldier," Keechie. They are indeed fighting a sort of war— against powers that divide and destroy. But it is also apparent in the thieves' code of thievery itself. And when such loyalties conflict, as they do in the moving conclusion of this novel, the results are shattering—even for little lives already shattered under a world full of thieves like us.

Thieves Like Us

THIEVES LIKE US

Chapter I

THERE was no doubt about it this time: over yonder behind the rise of scrub-oak, the automobile had left the highway and was laboring in low gear over the rutted road to where they waited. Like a saliva-wettened finger scorching across a hot iron, Bowie's insides spitted. He looked at Chicamaw.

Chicamaw's eyes were fixed up the weed-grown road, his thick-soled, convict shoes quiet on the rain-sprinkled earth that he had scarred with pacing. "That's him," he said.

Bowie looked behind him, across the creek's ridge of trees and over the field where the blades of the young corn glimmered like knives in the late-afternoon sun. Above the whitewashed walls of Alcatona Penitentiary reared the red-painted water-tank, the big cottonwood tree of the Upper Yard and the guards' towers.

The car was coming on. The jew's-harp twanging of the grasshoppers in the broomweeds seemed to heighten. I can rib myself up to do anything, Bowie thought. Anything. Every day in that place over there is wasted.

The car's springs creaked nearer. Bowie looked at Chicamaw again. "You're not planning on going some place, are you?"

Chicamaw did not move his head. "I'm just waitin' to see a horse about a feller," he said.

The taxicab bumped around the hill and wallowed toward them. Bowie squinted to see better. The figure in the back seat had on a straw hat. It was old T-Dub though. Come on, you cotton-headed old soldier!

The driver was that Kid that had been peddling marihuana to some of the boys. Jasbo they called him.

The cab stopped a few feet away and Bowie and Chicamaw moved toward it.

"Hello, Bowie," Jasbo said.

Bowie did not look at him. "Hi," he said.

T-Dub sat there with a big, paper-wrapped bundle across his knees. The yellow brightness of the new hat made his blond hair look like dry corn-silk.

"Well, what we waitin' on?" Chicamaw said. He opened the door.

2

T-Dub handed Chicamaw the bundle and then reached inside his blouse and pulled the gun. He scraped the barrel against the driver's cheek. "This is a stick-up, Jasbo," he said.

"Godamighty, Man," Jasbo said. His head quivered on a rigid neck.

Chicamaw ripped at the bundle strings and slapped at the paper. It contained blue denim overalls and white cotton shirts. He began stripping himself of his cotton-sacking prison clothing. Bowie and T-Dub began changing too.

Jasbo said: "Bowie, you know me. You tell these boys I'm all right."

"You just do what you're told," Bowie said.

"All you gotta do is tell me," Jasbo said.

Their clothing changed, Chicamaw pushed Jasbo over and got under the wheel and Bowie and T-Dub got in the back. They turned and went back up the road. On the highway, the wind began beating the speeding car like a hundred fly-swatters.

There was a car under the shed of the filling station on the right. A man in coveralls stood beside the red pump twisting the handle.

"Don't you let me see you throwing no winks, Jasbo," T-Dub said, "or I'll beat your ears down."

"I'll put my head 'tween my legs if you say so," Jasbo said.

They passed the filling station and Bowie looked back. The man was still twisting the pump handle. The empty highway behind looked like a stretching rubber band.

Bowie looked at the revolver in T-Dub's thick grasp. It was a silver-plated gun with a pearl handle. This old soldier knows what he is doing, Bowie thought. "Any rumbles in town?" he said.

T-Dub shook his head.

The highway still stretched emptily. They're finding out things back there now in the Warden's Office, Bowie thought. The Colonel's bowels are gettin' in an uproar now. Get out the stripes for that bunch of no-goods, he is saying. That's what you get for treatin' them like white men. No more baseball and passes to go fishing for that Bowie Bowers and Elmo Mobley. That T. W. Masefeld is not going to work in this prison commissary any more. Get out the dogs and the shotguns and the .30-30's and run them sons of bitches down. . . .

A car shot up over the rise ahead, hurtled toward them. It passed with a swooshing sound. Cars coming this way don't mean nothing, Bowie

4

thought. No more than them crows flying over yonder. T-Dub shifted the revolver to his left hand, wiped his palm on his thigh and regrasped the gun. Old T-Dub knows what he is doing.

The tendons of Chicamaw's lean neck played into two bony knots behind each ear. That Chicamaw knows what he is doing too. A man won't get in with two boys like this just every day. No more Time for any of them. They had shook on it.

The explosion was like the highway had snapped. The escaping air of the right back tire wailed. The car began to bump. On the left was a sign post: *Alcatona . . . 14 miles.* It was right in the middle of thirteen, Bowie thought. Old unlucky *thirteen*.

They bumped across the wooden bridge and moved up the dirt side road. When they were out of sight of the highway, Chicamaw stopped. The casing looked like it had been chopped with an ax. The spare was no good either.

Dusk was smoking out the ebbing glow on the horizon. Crickets in the roadside grass sounded like wind in loose telephone wires. Old unlucky *thirteen* is getting us up tight, Bowie thought. Hundred and twenty-two miles to Keota and Chicamaw's cousin, Dee Mobley and our Hole and *thirteen* riding our sore backs.

Chicamaw yanked at the barbed wire of the fence with the pliers and then came back with a strand. He lashed Jasbo to the steering wheel.

They moved now across the field of growing cotton toward the farmhouse light. "This gentleman up here might have a car with some tires on it," T-Dub said.

The earth of the field was soft and the tough stalks whipped their legs. In the distance, back toward the Prison, there was the sound of baying dogs and Bowie stopped. "Man, listen to them dogs," he said. Chicamaw and T-Dub halted. It was a vibrant, sonorous sound like the musical notes of a deep reed instrument.

"Hell, them's possum hounds," Chicamaw said.

They walked faster. The cottonwood stumps squatted in the field like headless toads. The farmhouse light glowed nearer, a fierce orange. T-Dub broke into a lope and Chicamaw and Bowie followed.

The woman with the baby in her arms led T-Dub and Bowie back to the lamp-lighted kitchen and the little man at the table half turned in his chair, a raw, bitten onion in his left hand, and looked up at them, at the gun in T-Dub's hand.

"We need that car out there of yours, Mister," T-Dub said. "Come on up."

Little Man turned and put the onion on the table. There were fried eggs and yellow corn bread on the plate. He got up and pushed the chair against the table. "Where's them keys, Mama?" he said.

The skin about Mama's mouth was twitching and her lower lip looked like it was going to melt on her chin. "I don't know," she said. The baby in her arms began to whimper.

Little Man found the keys in his pocket.

T-Dub looked at Mama. "Lady, if you like this gentleman here and want to see him again and I think you do, you just don't open your mouth after we leave."

"Yessir," Mama said. She began jogging the baby up and down. It began to cry.

Dust was as thick as silk on the car's body and there were chicken droppings on the hood and fenders. Little Man got in front with Chicamaw. "I haven't had this car out in more than a month," he said.

The highway paralleled the high embankment of

7

the Katy railroad now. Bowie watched the rising speedometer needle: *forty-five . . . fifty.* Stomp it, Chicamaw. Two pairs of nines riding our backs now. That kid Jasbo is squawking back yonder now all over the country. Ninety-nine years for highway robbery. Another pair for kidnaping.

The lights of the little highway town ahead spread with their approach and then scattered like flushed prey as they entered its limits. Under the filling-station sheds, swirling insects clouded the naked bulbs. The stores were closed; the depot dark. No Laws jumping us here, Bowie thought. No Square-Johns with shotguns. He turned toward T-Dub. "How many miles you think we done?"

"Twenty," T-Dub said.

"My woman has been pretty sick," Little Man said. "Been awful torn up lately."

Chicamaw's head went up and down.

Awful sick or scared, Bowie thought. District 'Cuter shouting that all over the Court House won't sound so good, boys. Stomp it, Chicamaw. Fog right up this line. Hour and forty minutes like this and we'll be cooling off with Real People. That Dee Mobley was Real People. Him and Chicamaw

8

had thieved together when they were kids. Chicamaw had been saving this Hole for eight years.

"Hasn't been well since the baby," Little Man
said.

The motor coughed, spluttered. Chicamaw
yanked out the choke button. The motor fired
again, missed; the cylinders pumped with furious
emptiness. Loose lugs rasped on the slowing wheels.

"Get her off the highway," T-Dub said. "Goose
her. Gentlemen, this wins the fur-lined bathtub."

Bowie, T-Dub and Little Man pushed, their feet
clopping on the pavement like horses. At last they
reached the crossroads and they pushed the car up
over the hump and out of sight of the highway.

Chicamaw started tying Little Man. T-Dub
breathed like he had asthma. "I've had plenty of
tough teaty in my day, but this is the toughest. I
might as well turn this .38 on me and do it up right."

A car was coming; its headlights glowed above the
hump. It sped on, its sound diminishing like the
roll of a muffled drum.

"Let's get moving," Chicamaw said.

They crossed the highway, crawled through the
fence and waded the hip-deep grass of the railroad

right-of-way. They climbed the embankment and got down on the railroad bed.

"We could flag a car and throw down on them?" Chicamaw said.

"To hell with them hot cars," T-Dub said. "I'll walk it."

"We can do it by just keeping right down these ties," Chicamaw said.

"Like goddamned hoboes," T-Dub said.

The moon hung in the heavens like a shred of fingernail. There was only the sound of their feet crunching in the gravel. Chicamaw led.

The rails began to murmur. It was a train behind them. After a while, the locomotive's light showed, tiny as a lightning bug. It began to swell.

They climbed up the cut's side, clutching at the grass, and on top lay down. The earth began trembling as if the cut's sides were going to cave in and carry them under the wheels. The pounding wheels of the freight-train thundered and crashed and, after a long time, the twin red lights of the caboose passed.

"I wouldn't of minded holding that down for a while," T-Dub said.

"Why didn't you holler for them to stop, Bowie?" Chicamaw said.

"I didn't want to make them mad at us," Bowie said.

The nail in the heel of Bowie's right shoe was digging now into the flesh. To hell with it, he thought. Bad start is a good ending, boys. You can't throw snake-eyes all day. Box-cars won't jump up in your face every throw. There's a natural for us up this road.

.   .   .   .   .

Bowie came out of his sleep with T-Dub's voice, deep as a cistern's echo and Chicamaw's muffled rattle still stroking his ears. His feet felt like the toenails had been drawn out and the bits ground in his heels. The sun was piercing the plum thicket like ice picks and when Bowie turned on his back he placed his forearm over his eyes.

"I cased that bank in Zelton four times," T-Dub said. "It was a bird's nest on the ground, but every time something came up. Maybe this time will be different."

"I'm ready for a piece of it myself," Chicamaw said.

"I tell you one thing," T-Dub said. "When I rob my next bank it will be my twenty-eighth."

"I hope it's twenty-nine in a couple of weeks."

Bowie's insides quivered. I can rib myself up to do anything, he thought.

"These kids trying to rob these banks are just ding-bats," T-Dub said. "They'll charge a bank with a filling station across the street and a telephone office above and a hardware store next door."

"You got to watch them upstairs offices across the street from a bank too," Chicamaw said. "There's lawyers and doctors and people with shotguns just waiting for a bank to be robbed."

"I'm not going to fool with any of these clod-hopper town banks," Chicamaw said. "You got to work just as hard for a thousand out of one of them as you do in a good one for fifty."

"Pick you a bank that's a depository for the county and city and you're going to find a set-up," T-Dub said. "That's why I say it don't hurt to case a bank for a week before you charge it."

Five thousand dollars and I'm backing off, Bowie thought. Five thousand salted away and I'm going back to Alky. I've done so much Time that I can do a couple of more on my ear. Go back there and grin at them from ear to ear. I can twist that Warden around my little finger. He's all right though.

He'll close them books on me and my record will be clean in a couple of years. Then I'll buy me a mouthpiece for a couple of thousand that's got friends in the Capital and you'll see me coming out of that Alky squared up and with a stake.

The best way to case the Inside of a bank, T-Dub said, was by going in and cashing twenty-dollar bills. In Florida he had opened up an account in a bank just to big-eye it good.

Bowie sat up.

"The Country Boy is up," Chicamaw said. His teeth were as white as the pearl of a gun butt.

There were tiny lights in T-Dub's eyes, gray as .30-30 bullets. "What do you want for supper, Bowie? Plums or fried chicken?"

Bowie looked at a ripened plum on the stem above his head. "I'll take plums," he said.

Chicamaw had his trousers rolled to his knees and now he was pinching into his hair-matted legs.

"What the hell are you doing?" Bowie said.

"Red bugs," Chicamaw said.

Bowie looked at his blood-crusted feet; at the curled toes and grass-filled wrinkles of his shoes. Just one more night of walking though. Just a half a night. He lay back down.

13

Chicamaw was talking now about a bank he robbed in Kansas. "I knew I hadn't sacked up no more than two thousand out of that nigger-head and I just happened to pick up that cash slip. You know that one they put in every night to show how much cash they got on hand? . . . Well, it didn't jibe with what I had so I went back up to that Dutchman and I says to him: 'Friend, have I got everything around here?' He says: 'You got every bit of it.' I says: 'Is your cash receipt slip usually right?' He says: 'Why, yes.' I says: 'Well, I haven't got but two thousand here and this slip shows four thousand eight hundred and sixty-two dollars. Now cough it up.' That guy began swearing up and down so I just put the twitch to him. His eyes turned as red as any red you ever did see."

Bowie sat back up. "What's a twitch?" he said.

"Don't worry, you'll see one pretty soon. When I work I always carry myself one. Get you a piece of window cord and make a little stick with a hole in it and fix a loop and just put that around a man's head and give it a twist and he's gonna think his brains are coming out his ears. Anyway, this Dutchman hollers calf rope and he shows me the bottom drawer of a desk there. Sure enough, right there in it, was four little packs of the prettiest *five hundred-* and *one hundred-*dollar bills you ever saw."

A gust of wind combed the thicket and bent the stretch of high Johnston grass that separated them from the railroad. Bowie lay back.

"You know what that banker would have done if you hadn't of got onto that slip," T-Dub said. "He'd of squawked that he had been robbed of it all just the same. There's more of these bankers than you can shake a stick at that's got it stacked around over their banks and just praying every day to be robbed."

"Sure," Chicamaw said.

"They're thieves just like us," T-Dub said.

Bowie flecked an ant off the back of his hand. I'm not going to get in this too deep, gentlemen. You going to see this white child backing off when he's got five thousand.

The feet of T-Dub and Chicamaw scraped in sudden violence and Bowie jerked up like a jack-knife. He looked toward the two. They were looking into the Johnston grass. T-Dub had the gun in his hand.

Bowie watched. Something was moving in that

15

grass yonder all right. It wasn't wind either. He picked up his shoes. The grass parted again!

Chicamaw led the way, plunging through the thicket like a football half-back; T-Dub behind and Bowie following barefooted and carrying his shoes. They did not stop running until they reached the woods. Then they stopped and looked back toward the thicket.

"What did you-all see?" Bowie said. "Jesus Christ."

"Something was in that grass," Chicamaw said.

"If there wasn't I left a damned good three-dollar hat over there," T-Dub said. "I can see your socks hanging from here, Bowie."

"I thought all the Laws in the county were in that grass the way you-all tore out," Bowie said.

"I'll bet it was a hog or something," T-Dub said. "Turkey or something. I'll bet any amount you guys want to name."

"If you think it's just a hog why don't you just trot back over there and get that hat?" Chicamaw said.

"Ah, I want to go bare-headed anyway. Like these jelly beans."

Bowie sat down and began putting on his shoes. His feet were bleeding again.

"Think you going to make it, Bowie?" T-Dub said.

"The way I come across over here looks like I could run it," Bowie said.

Chapter II

THAT rain-blurred sprinkle of lights yonder was
Keota. Before the rain commenced, Bowie had heard
sounds of the town, but now there was only the
smacking of the wind-driven rain against the shocks
of old wheat around him and its clatter on the stub-
bled earth. He had been alone now more than two
hours and it must be getting along toward three or
four o'clock. In the black depths underneath those
lights yonder, T-Dub and Chicamaw were looking
for Dee Mobley's place. When they found Chicamaw's cousin, they were coming back after him.
Three flashes of the headlamps, if they got Dee's car,
would be the signal.

Bowie reached down now and pressed his numb
feet. They felt like stumps. A man on stumps
couldn't do much good if he was jumped and that is
why he had stayed here to wait.

The thunder in the east rumbled nearer and then
cracked above him in a jagged prong of lightning.

The flash bared the sodden stretch to the sagging fence and road.

I won't be hearing any more from my people, Bowie thought. Mama. Aunt Pearl. Cousin Tom. Goodbye to you people. The first thing the Law does is look up the people a man has been writing to and watch them places.

Goodbye, Mama. There's one thing about you. Whatever I ever did was all right with you. This is the only way. Maybe you'll be getting an envelope with three or four hundred dollars in it pretty soon and then you can go off and get that pellagra cured up. Get away from that husband you got for a while.

So long, Cousin Tom. Thanks for them letters and cigarettes. But all the cheering in the world don't help you none, Pal, when you're in a place like that back yonder. You know every day what is going to happen the next.

Aunt Pearl, you're a fine woman, but all the Christian Scientist stuff in the world don't help you none if you haven't got the money to buy a lawyer. And to get a good one you got to have good money.

Approaching car lights bobbed on the road and Bowie got up. The laboring machine plowed the

mud of the road right on past. Bowie lowered himself back to the ground.

Them boys will be back here. Takes time to
locate a man when you don't know where he lives.
Let him stay out here? Them boys weren't made
that way. It was getting doggone late though.
There wasn't a dozen lights in the town now.

Lightning slashed the swirling heavens. Maybe a
man saw something like that when they kicked the
switch off on you in the Chair, Bowie thought. It
didn't seem like no nine years since that morning
when his lawyer came and told him they weren't
going to burn him. Maybe though he had died back
there in the Chair? This was just his Spirit out here
in this rain? In this old world, anything happened.
Maybe I'm like a cat with nine lives. I done lost one
of them back there in that Alky Chair. Eight more
to go. . . . Look here, Bowie, old boy, snap out of
it. You're going to go ding-batty out here.

Another car was coming. It sounded like a
Model-T; had one twitching feeble light.

Bowie moved toward the fence in a half crouch.
The car was a Ford pick-up, its body boards thumping and rattling. That light on it was either just
going off and on or signaling. What was it doing?

He checked the shout in his throat. The car went on, the sound of its straining motor dying in the night.

He sat now at the side of the road. It couldn't be very long until daybreak. Well, I can't sit out here up into the day. Them boys must have got a rumble over there. They might be in trouble this very minute. They wouldn't leave me out here though. Not them boys. We've had our heads together too long on this business. Take old T-Dub. Him knocking down in that Commissary every day so they would have a stake. A man didn't start out with money that come that hard with two fellows and not intend to go through with it. Not any four hundred and twenty-five dollars. And planning as far ahead as they had? Cooling off at Dee's and then going on down into Texas and getting hold of T-Dub's sister-in-law and getting her to get them a furnished house. Nosir, that boy just wasn't made that way. And Chicamaw? Them white teeth.

The rain slapped his face and crawled on his numb feet. But I can't stay out here forever. If they ain't here by daybreak, I've just got to go on in. I can't help it. I'm going in.

.　　.　　.　　.　　.

The harnessed mules plowed the road's muck toward Bowie, pulling a wagon with a tarpaulin as gray and soggy as the morning. The driver, his drooping straw sombrero bowed against the drizzle, slopped along at the wagon's side. His overalls were rolled to his calves and hunks of mud leaped from his moving shoes. Now the sombrero raised.

"Good morning, Friend," Bowie said.

Sombrero shifted the wad of tobacco in his jaws. "Mornin'," he said.

Bowie pointed at his shoes. "Mind if I hang on the back of your wagon into town? My feet have plumb played out on me."

Sombrero nodded toward the wagon's rear. "Climb up in it if you want to."

Bowie went around and climbed through the canvas flap and into the wagon. The smell of alfalfa was dry and clean. He saw now the woman and the little boy. They sat on quilt-covered straw against the seat.

"Your man said I could pile in here, Lady?"

The woman nodded.

Bowie leaned back against the sides, stretched his feet in guarded relaxation. The wagon's movement was soothing and its clean dryness began to sponge him like a dry chamois skin. He closed his eyes.

"Who's that man, Ma?"

Bowie opened his eyes, looked at the child and grinned. "You don't mind me riding with you, do you, Son?"

The boy burrowed his face against his mother's bosom and she patted him. "He's a friend of your pappy's, honey."

The hoofs of the mules began clopping and Bowie asked the woman: "We in town?"

The woman nodded. "On the Square."

Bowie edged feet forward to the wagon's end, parted the flap and slid out. The pavement was like a cushion of pins.

In the center of the Square was the Court House, a two-story sandstone building with big basement signs: *Whites . . . Colored.* One- and two-story buildings fenced the Square: *Greenberg's Dry Goods Store . . . Keota State Bank . . . Rexall Drug Store . . . Hamburger's 5 & 10¢.*

The rain had stopped and the sun looked like a circle of wet, yellow paper. Bowie walked across the Court House lawn toward the dry goods store on the corner.

The clerk leaned against the doorway with his arms folded across his chest and when Bowie neared he pushed with his shoulder blades and stood erect. "Yessir?" he said.

"I got ten bucks, Pardner," Bowie said, "and I got to have a pair of pants and a shirt and socks and shoes and some short-handled drawers."

"We'll see," Pardner said.

Bowie followed him back into the gloom and deeper into the smell of damp wool and bolted goods and floor sweep. Pardner turned on a fly-specked bulb above a table of khaki work pants.

In dry clothing now, Bowie sat on a bench while Pardner laced the new shoes on his feet. "You don't know a feller around here by the name of Tobey or Hobby or something like that, do you?" he asked.

Pardner cocked his head. "Don't believe I do."

"I used to know a feller up in Tulsy who settled down here. Been in this town a pretty good while I understand. Mobby or something like that."

"What does he look like?"

Bowie described Chicamaw. "Oh, he's sort of an Indian looking feller. Come up to about my shoulders. Black eyes and pretty skinny."

Pardner shook his head.

"He was working in a filling station up in Tulsy."

"There's a fellow named Mobley out on the Dallas highway that's got a little store and station out there."

"It wasn't Mobley, I'm sure of that."

"Did he have a girl named Keechie, little Indian-looking girl?"

"No. It don't matter. I didn't know him so well."

The new shoes made his feet feel like they were not even sore. It was good to walk. The sun was blotting the puddles and making the dry stretches of the highway glare. He passed the lumber yard with its fence of shredded show posters, the closed cotton gin, the tourist camp: *Kozy Komfort Kamp*.

That was the place yonder all right. That station right yonder with the orange-colored pump. A man sat under the shed in a tilted chair. Back of the station was a smokehouse-looking structure and then woods. Farther up the highway, on the left side, was another station.

Bowie went up under the shed toward the man in the tilted chair. "How you do, Friend?" Bowie said.

"Howdy," the man said. He had a heavy face, rough as oak bark and long, black sideburns touched with wiry gray. The black cotton shirt had white buttons.

"Got a cold soda?" Bowie said.

The man got up and lifted the lid of the ice-box and Bowie reached in and picked up a bottle.

Bowie saw now the girl standing behind the screened doorway of the store. She was dark and small and her high pointed breasts stretched the blue cotton of the polo shirt.

Bowie looked at the man. "I wonder if I could see you private a minute?"

The man looked toward the girl and she went away.

"You're Dee Mobley, aren't you?"

"That's me."

"You haven't had a couple of visitors lately?"

Mobley looked at Bowie's shoes. "You got on some new shoes there, haven't you? Feet been hurting?"

"You doggone whistling. I just got these up town."

"New pants too?"

Bowie grinned.

"Where in the hell," Mobley said, "have *you* been?"

"Waiting for that Chicamaw and that T-Dub Masefeld."

"I went after you last night myself," Mobley said. "Raining cats and nigger babies."

"In a Model-T truck?"

"That was me."

"Well, I'll be— Can you beat that. And I just sat out there and let you go by."

Mobley made a thumbing motion toward the filling station up the highway. Two figures in uniform coveralls sat on a bench under its shed. "Them Square-Johns up yonder are always big-eyeing this way so you just go on past like you were hitch-hiking and then cut back through the woods. The boys are in that bunk of mine right back of this place."

Bowie dog-trotted through the woods toward the filling station. He could see the place that Dee called his bunk. It had a corrugated iron roof and the limbs of a big pecan tree shaded it. He crawled through the fence and went to the bunk's door and knocked. The springs of a bed inside creaked a little. He knocked again. There was no answer. "Chicamaw," he called.

Feet thumped on the floor inside, stomped toward

28

the door. T-Dub's face was framed in the parted door. "For Christ's sake, come in," he said.

Chicamaw lay on the iron bed in his underwear. "We thought maybe you had gone back to Alky."

"I just been swimming that's all," Bowie said. "And thinking I was a lone wolf."

"I was going to go back out there tonight myself," Chicamaw said.

T-Dub pointed at the bare wooden table. On it was a bowl of pork and beans, a hunk of yellow cheese and a broken loaf of bread. "You want to glom?"

"Man, I'll say."

"We didn't get holed up here until five o'clock this morning," Chicamaw said. "I was going to go back after you tonight. I don't see how Dee missed you."

"It was my fault," Bowie said. He poured beans on a hunk of the bread and pressed it into a sandwich. He took a bite and chewed and grinned.

Chapter III

UP UNTIL a year ago, Dee Mobley had been boot-legging corn whisky, but the new Sheriff in Keota had it in for him, he said. He squatted now against the wall of the Bunk, his breath as strong as rubbing-alcohol fumes, a finger-rolled cigarette wagging on his lower lip. "The Sheriff likes these druggist boys here," Dee said. "They're doing all the booze busi-ness here now."

"Them Laws and druggists are thieves just like us," T-Dub said. He drew his hand across his sweat-beaded forehead and his fingers made a clicking sound as he slung it on the floor. "It's getting so a man has to have a gun to make a piece of money."

The afternoon sun was packing heat into the low-ceilinged, crowded room. Chicamaw sat on an up-turned bucket filing on the barrels of the .12-gauge shotgun with a hack saw. Bowie lay on the bed, a wet towel across his face.

The druggists were fixing up the cheap trade with jake and orange peel and hair tonics, Dee said, and the Indians were buying their canned heat at the five & ten. Doctors were getting the good business with prescriptions.

Dee said he had been running the grocery and filling station since fall. His daughter Keechie helped him. She stayed up in town with his sister Mara, and he stayed in the Bunk here at nights.

"That girl of yours sure mean-eyed me this morning when she brought that grub out here," T-Dub said. "I don't think she likes us around here worth a doggone."

"She don't have much to do with nobody," Dee said.

Bowie took the towel off his face so he could see Dee.

"She'll take care of you while I'm up in Tulsy," Dee said. "Just you boys don't go around in front of the station and be careful about lights at night."

T-Dub counted out three hundred and twenty-five dollars and gave it to Dee. This was to buy a second-hand car in Tulsa, cover ten dollars for the shotgun and twenty-five for Dee's trouble.

"I might be able to make it back by tomorrow night," Dee said. "But if I see I'm going to get in here after daylight I'll just wait until the next night."

"We'd like to shell out of here about eight o'clock at night," T-Dub said.

"We don't forget our friends, Dee," Chicamaw said. "You do the best you can for us and when we get in some real money, you're liable to see a piece of it."

After Dee left, T-Dub said they had ninety-five dollars left. It had to take them to Texas and pay a month's rent on a furnished house.

Chicamaw put the shotgun down and went over and picked up a road map on the bed.

T-Dub said the best way to leave a Hole was early in the evening when the traffic was heaviest. Stay off the main highways as much as you could and follow timbered country. Keep a couple of five-gallon cans filled with gasoline and circle cities like Dallas and Fort Worth where the Laws had them scout cars and radios.

The wheels of a truck ground in the gravel of the station's driveway and they listened. Bottles rattled. "Soda-pop truck," Bowie said.

"I can run these roads all day and night through," T-Dub said. "Just keep your car clean and not let it look like it was being run hard and everybody stay shaved up and looking like you were just a fellow about town. I can count it on my hand the times I been jumped on the road."

"Just give me one man driving and me sitting in the back with a .30-30 and I can hold off any carload of Laws that ever took out after anybody," Chicamaw said.

"You can do it with a nigger-shooter," T-Dub said. "I don't see where these fellows they call G-men, them Big Shots, get that stuff about thieves not having no guts. I don't see how they get that."

"Me neither," Bowie said. "They don't do anything unless they got ten carloads and when they jump anybody they use about fourteen hundred rounds of ammunition.'"

"Laws never did worry me," T-Dub said. "It's the fellers you thought were your friends that beats you. And a woman mad at you. They are what beat you."

"Liquor too," Bowie said. "Some guys have to be stewed to the gills before they can work. Me, I want my head clear when I start out."

"Whiss will do it all right," T-Dub said. "But a woman mad at you can get you in a rank quicker than anything. Yessir, the Laws would be up tight if it wasn't for sore women and snitches."

"They're full of rabbit all right, them Laws," Chicamaw said.

"I wouldn't trust Jesus Christ," Bowie said.

"Listen to old Country Boy," Chicamaw said.

"Even if I saw Jesus Christ walking right in this place I wouldn't trust him," Bowie said.

The heat was getting more intense. It stuffed Bowie's nostrils and seared high up in his nose. He took the towel and soaked it again in the bucket of water.

Chicamaw started taking off his overalls.

"You ought not to do that," Bowie said. "No tellin' when that girl might come out here."

Chicamaw resnapped the overall straps.

"I'd sure like to let that sister-in-law of mine know I'm coming," T-Dub said. "But that's a good way to get a rumble. Writing letters. We'll just go on to MacMasters and I'll get her on the phone."

Chicamaw looked up from the road map. "It's three hundred and twenty-five miles from here. That country is sure bald out in there. Nothing but oil-wells and mesquite trees."

"Plenty of roads though," T-Dub said. "Man, I was raised in that West Texas country."

"I guess you know that sister-in-law of yours pretty good?" Chicamaw said.

"She's Real People," T-Dub said. "A woman that has stuck by that bud of mine like she has isn't going to turn down a chance to make some money. That bud of mine can be sprung out of Texas with a couple of thousand. He's just doing five years. On a two-for-one job now. And that woman of his is going to do all she can."

"Zelton is forty miles from MacMasters," Chicamaw said. "That's where we going to get the house, uh?"

"There's mighty nice banks in both of those towns, but Zelton, I think, takes my eye first."

Chicamaw folded the map. "I know a mouthpiece in MacMasters," he said. "Name Hawkins. Archibald J. Hawkins. Old Windy we called him. Him and me were holed up together in Mexico for a year. There's one old boy that sure beat the Law."

"What did he do?" Bowie said.

"He was a county treasurer right there in MacMasters and he sacked himself up twenty or twenty-five thousand just knocking down every month and then things started gettin' hot and he rabbited to Mexico."

"Unlatched a vault?" Bowie asked.

"Oh, no. Just knocking down. He bought all the County's stuff, see. Gravel and machinery and things like that. He would make out a voucher for five loads of gravel when he had bought only one and then go down to the bank and cash it and pocket the other four. He was in Mexico for fourteen years. All the witnesses died or forgot and then he went back just as big as you please. And on top of that took the bar examination and is practising law right there now."

"Them politicians are thieves just like us," T-Dub said. "Only they got more sense and use their damned tongues instead of a gun."

"If you ever need a mouthpiece," Chicamaw said, "Old Windy wouldn't be bad."

"I'm not needing any more lawyers myself," T-Dub said. "The way I figure is that when they get me again I won't be in any shape for a lawyer or anything else in this world to do me any good."

"That's me," Bowie said. "I mean to get me out of any new trouble."

"Well, the way I figure it," Chicamaw said, "is

that two and two make five and if at first you don't suck seed, keep on sucking 'til you do suck seed."

"Aw, you damned Indian," Bowie said.

.   .   .   .   .

The voice of the girl, Keechie, made Bowie's veins distend and there was a velvety, fluttering sensation in his spine. She was squatting over there now by the Bunk's kerosene heater, the brown flannel of her skirt stretched tight across her bottom, showing T-Dub how to keep the wick from smoking. T-Dub had tried to boil coffee on it this morning and had only succeeded in filling everybody's noses full of soot and blacking the underwear Bowie had washed.

"Just wipe it off with a match like this," Keechie said.

"That's one thing old T-Dub don't know nothing about," Chicamaw said.

Keechie got up, holding her blackened hands out. Bowie snatched the towel off the bed post and held it toward her. "It's pretty dirty," he said.

Keechie took the towel. "Thank you."

"That big Country Boy is some gallant, ain't he, Keechie?" Chicamaw said.

Bowie's ears felt like the velvet was being pressed

against them now. "Don't pay no attention to that ignoramus," he said.

"Were you raised in the country?" Keechie said.

Bowie shook his head. "Don't pay no attention to them two."

"He's just hard-headed, Miss Keechie," T-Dub said. "That's all."

"Soft-headed," Chicamaw said.

"His head looks all right to me," Keechie said.

Bowie tried hard not to swallow. "All right, you guys, that's enough."

Keechie pointed at the bed. On it was a filled paper sack and two folded newspapers. "There's some canned soup in that sack and you can heat it on that stove now." She turned toward the door.

"Thanks for the grub and papers, Miss Keechie," T-Dub said.

Bowie looked at her, the black hair, cut like a boy's; the short, strong neck and compact shoulders. "Sure thank you," he said.

"Forget it," Keechie said. She went out the door.

"That little girl don't think any too much of us, I'm here to tell you," T-Dub said. He went over to the bed and picked up a newspaper.

"She's all right," Chicamaw said. "Just stuck up."

"She acts like a little soldier to me," Bowie said.

"Old Dee just lets her do him anyway," Chicamaw said. "He won't never go on a real toot around here any more. If he wants to get boiled, he'll go clear up to Muskogee. That man's got a right to drink though. Wife leaving him like she did."

"Keechie's mother?" Bowie said.

"She run off with some damned guy. Running a medicine show."

"That little girl hasn't got no business around a bunch of criminals like us," Bowie said.

"Man, lookee here," T-Dub said. He had the Oklahoma City newspaper spread out on the bed and was tapping the left top column. "Just lookee here."

Bowie went over and he and Chicamaw looked:

ALCATONA, Okla., Sept. 15—The escape of three life-term prisoners who kidnaped a taxicab driver and a farmer in their desperate flight was announced here tonight by Warden Everett Gaylord of the State Penitentiary. Combined forces of prison, County and City officers were looking for the trio. The fugitives are:

Elmo (Three-Toed) Mobley, 35, bank robbery; T. W. (Tommy Gun) Masefeld, 44, bank robbery and Bowie A. Bowers, 27, murder.

"Pulling that toe stuff again on me," Chicamaw said. "All right, you sons of bitches."

Mobley and Bowers, Warden Gaylord disclosed, took advantage of permits allowing them to go fishing on prison property and Masefeld of a pass to town. All three were privileged trusties.

Jed Miracle, 21, Alcatona taxi driver, was bound in his own taxi which the fugitives abandoned after a tire blew out. E. T. Waters, farmer living at the edge of Akota, twelve miles south of here, gave descriptions of three men who commandeered his car at the point of a gun. After traveling with the trio for more than an hour, the fuel of the car was exhausted and Waters was tied and abandoned in his own car like Miracle.

The desperate trio are believed to be headed for the hills of Eastern Oklahoma where so many criminals have found refuge in the past few years.

Bowers, youngest of the escaped men, was serving a life sentence that had been commuted from the death penalty. He was convicted in the murder of a store-keeper in Selpa County when he was 18 years old. The killing took place during an attempted robbery. He was a member of the prison baseball team.

All of the men had good prison records, Warden Gaylord said. Masefeld had charge of the prison commissary, selling cigarettes and candies to the inmates. He had been in the prison six years. Mobley, also a member of the prison ball team, had served five years of a 99 year sentence from Larval County.

Miracle, the cab driver, described tonight how he was lured to the creek a mile from the prison by Masefeld and forced at the point of a gun to surrender his cab and accompany them.

"Masefeld told me in town he wanted to take some sandwiches and soda pop out to some friends of his who were fishing," Miracle declared. "I had done that plenty of times for some of the trusty boys and I did not think anything about it. When we reached the place, Masefeld jabbed the gun in my back and said he would kill me if I did not obey him," Miracle asserted.

"A tire blew out," Miracle went on, "and the extra was down too, so they tied me up and went on across a cotton field toward the highway. I managed to work myself loose and drove the car back to town."

The shouts of Waters, the farmer kidnaped by the men, attracted coon hunters who freed him. He declared the men treated him courteously.

"That toe stuff," Chicamaw said.

"It tickles me," T-Dub said, "about this Tommy Gun they're putting on me. I never did have but one machine gun in my life and I never did even try it out. I'll take an automatic pump gun any old day."

"It's not a very long piece about us though, is it?" Chicamaw said.

"Brother, I wish it was just two lines," Bowie said.

"Nothing at all you mean," T-Dub said. "Papers can raise more heat than anything. These Laws work like hell to get their names in the papers."

·   ·   ·   ·   ·

42

They lolled on the ground in front of the Bunk, unrecognizable bundles in the darkness, only their slapping and blowing at mosquitoes interrupting the quiet. This was the second night they had waited on Dee Mobley. The lights of the station had not been turned on this evening. Everything was set to take off. Chicamaw had the shotgun sawed off so he could carry it underneath the old lumberjacket Dee had given him. Keechie had two five-gallon cans of gasoline filled up in front of the station, two sacks of groceries and three cotton-picking sacks.

"I just hope it's not the car that's holding him up," T-Dub said. "I'll be damned if I start out in a wreck."

"He's probably drinking a little," Chicamaw said.

Bowie got up and stretched. "I wish he had picked some other time to drink if that's it." He walked over to the edge of the tree's inky shadow and stood there, looking at the back of the station. Then he came back and stood above Chicamaw and T-Dub. They were quiet again.

Bowie moved up the side of the station and peered around under the shed. He saw the figure sitting in the chair by the ice-box and his shoes rasped in the gravel with his start.

43

"My goodness," he said. "I didn't know that was you."

"That's all right," Keechie said.

He cleared his throat. "I didn't know anybody was around here."

"That's all right."

He looked at the Model-T pick-up parked just off the driveway. "I was thinking though that I hadn't heard it leave."

"No," Keechie said.

Bowie moved toward her.

"Sit down if you want to," Keechie said.

He lowered himself to the bottom of the doorway. There was a car under the shed of the brightly lighted filling station up the highway. Two men were standing beside it and watching the attendant fill the tank. "I don't know what could be holding that Daddy of yours," he said.

"I have an idea. If it had to be done I should have done it."

Bowie shook his head. "We don't have any business around here anyway."

The lights of a car popped around the curve from town, sprayed the highway with luminous foam.

Bowie strained back against the door screen. The car passed.

"I read it in the paper about you," Keechie said.

Bowie's head went up and down.

"I guess you thought you had to leave?"

"I didn't see any use of doing any more Time. It wasn't getting me anywhere. All that was keeping me in there was money."

Keechie shook her head. "You won't get anywhere like this. Not with company like that back yonder."

"I don't know," Bowie said. "What will be, will be."

"That Chicamaw wouldn't be anything else if he could."

"I think you got them boys down wrong now. You take old T-Dub. He's got him a little farm picked out already up in Kentucky. He wants to settle down."

"That Chicamaw Mobley has never liked anything but trouble all his life."

Bowie grinned. "He's a little wild all right."

The car under the shed of the other filling station drove away. The attendant went back and sat on the bench.

"If I wasn't so hot I'd like to have me a filling station," Bowie said. "Now what I would like to have is a tourist camp."

"That would be too slow for you," Keechie said. "You want to live your life fast."

"You got me down wrong, Keechie. You'd see me following a one-eyed mule and a Georgia walking stock if I had to and what's more, like it. If I could."

Keechie took a pack of cigarettes from her polo shirt pocket, pushed up one and offered it to Bowie. When he touched her hand, the velvety glow stiffened his blood. The lighted cigarette trembled between his fingers.

"How come you to ever get in trouble?" Keechie said.

"I never was in but one."

"That one."

"You mean the Chair?"

"Yes."

"Just some fellows on the carnival I was traveling with said they knew how to make some money and I just sort of went along to see how it was done. I wanted to get some money so I could go up to Colorado and join another show. Them boys had a safe picked out and I just went along."

"You were on a carnival?"

"I went on it when I was fourteen.   Just rousta-boutin'."

"Did you run away from home?"

"I just left.   Year after Dad died."

"Your Dad is dead?"

"Killed.   Man killed him."

Shoes crunched at the side of the station and Bowie's head jerked.   It was Chicamaw.   "I wondered what had become of you?"

"Just talking," Bowie said.

"Don't let me bother you."   Chicamaw went on back.

Keechie flipped the cigarette toward the pick-up and Bowie watched its glow on the dark ground.

"Did you shoot that man in Selpa?" Keechie said.

"It was me or him," Bowie said.   "He was coming around the car after me with a gun."

The chair under Keechie creaked a little as she moved.

"If I had run like the others I wouldn't be this way now.   The guy that knew all about robbing safes was the first one to run.   The Big Shot."

Keechie took another cigarette.

"You smoke a lot," he said.

47

"I don't want it." She broke it in her hand.

"I know a man can't last Out Here long. But I'm not going to try and last. I'm going to back off and it isn't going to be long. I can still square myself up."

"No," Keechie said. "You can't beat it this way."

"Deep down in me I know I can't, but I myself says I can."

Another car was coming around the curve. Suddenly, its lights were flooding the shed under which they sat. Neither moved.

It was a coupe and Dee. He got out of the car awkwardly. He was drunk all right. "Hadtufftime," he said.

Bowie went back and told Chicamaw and T-Dub. "You think it's too late to start tonight?" he said.

"Hell, no," Chicamaw said. He and T-Dub went in the Bunk.

The motor of the Model-T around in front fired and Bowie started moving fast toward the shed. When he got around there, the pick-up was already on the highway. He watched it go, listening to the sound of the motor perishing in the darkness.

T-Dub and Chicamaw were piling things in the

car. "Where's them cotton-picking sacks?" T-Dub said.

"I got them," Bowie said. He went over to the chair where she had been sitting and picked up the sacks.

"Hadtufftime," Dee said. "Tufftime."

They drove off. Shortly the wind was whipping the sacks on the fenders and insects swirled in the lamp beams and splattered on the windshield.

Chapter IV

THE two five-gallon cans rattled emptily in the coupe's rear and the red level of the gasoline gauge was below the half mark, but Fort Worth and Dallas were behind now, given the run-around without a rumble. One hundred and forty miles out this straight stretch and they would be in MacMasters. Bowie was driving.

On this side of MacMasters, at an old, abandoned wildcat well that T-Dub had described, Bowie and Chicamaw were getting out and T-Dub was going on in to contact his sister-in-law. Just as soon as he got a house, he would come back and get them.

They talked about houses now. When they had about five places, T-Dub said, and all had good hotel-lobby fronts, he would say they had a real set-up. He wanted a house in Zelton and another one in Gusherton. Then one in that resort town, Clear Waters, and one in Lothian and Twin Montes. These towns were within a radius of two hundred miles and not more than an hour's driving apart.

A house in each of them would give you a Hole that you could be cooling off in within an hour after a bank was sacked.

Always get places with double garages, T-Dub said, and keep the cars out of sight. And never let the neighbors see more than one man at a time. And don't let anybody ever do any questioning. If there was any questioning, you do it yourself. Now up here in Zelton and Gusherton, they could be lease buyers or promoters as soon as they got good fronts.

"We're cotton pickers tonight and look it," Chicamaw said. "How much cotton can you pick a day, Country Boy?"

"Oh, a pound if I worked real hard," Bowie said. He looked at the fuel mark. It was getting damned low.

"And another thing," T-Dub said. "Always give the landlady the best of the deal. Keep her satisfied."

"I had me a landlady down in Florida," Chicamaw said, "and I want you to know that there was one woman that could drink me under the table. There wasn't anything that woman wouldn't do. And just when everything was going smooth with us, they got me."

T-Dub started telling about a house he had in Colorado. The damnedest, smallest thing got him in a rank there, this right arm almost shot off and a big Law with a double-barreled shotgun jamming it in his eyes and him standing there and not even able to lift his arms. The thing he had done though was going off and staying a couple of weeks and not telling the milkman. That bastard got scared over a couple of dollars and he went to the woman that owned the house. She went over to the house and saw it all locked up and she just went in. She got an eyeful. He had that damned machine gun in that house and a bunch of shells. She goes to the Law and they show her a bunch of pictures and sure enough she picks him out. The Laws sit around that house and here he comes back. They would have killed him if it hadn't been for a woman on the porch of a house across the street. She got to shouting and screaming and telling the Laws to stop or they would have killed him. He had them black eyes where that big yellow bastard poked him with that shotgun for a month and a half.

"We sure got to stop and gas up pretty soon," Bowie said.

"That state of Colorado though," T-Dub said.

"You ain't never going to get me back in it. They were going to try and put the Chair on me up there. I was praying for Oklahoma to come and get me. They had me positively identified in that state anyway. This Colorado 'cuter was after me right now and I just figured that I had been unlucky enough to draw him and I wasn't going to be lucky enough to beat that Chair. There was a little old auditor that used to come around to us boys in them death cells and talk. Kind of wanted to write pieces for the magazines or something. I got to feeling him out and finally I just showed him a *five-hundred* dollar bill. I had carried that in the sole of my shoe for six months. He tumbles and brings me a .25 automatic and some tape too just like I asked. I taped that right between my legs and Man, I was set. I had made up my mind that if they went ahead and started putting that Chair on me I was going to kill everybody around me that was man enough to die."

"They didn't even try you up there though, did they?" Chicamaw said.

"Naw. That's how come me to be back in Alky. Oklahoma finally come and got me. A little old jailer up here in the Panhandle took that gun off of me. I'd been trying to get rid of it for a two weeks."

The highway turned in a banking curve and then down the highway they could see the scattered lights of a small, sleeping town. "We got to gas up here," Bowie said.

Everything was closed in the town. Small globes burned in the rears of the stores, over the sacks of grain, the cans of oil and tire tubes in the filling stations and the show-cases in the hardware store.

"Looks like we going to have to wake somebody up," T-Dub said.

"We can just unlatch one ourselves," Chicamaw said.

Bowie drove under the shed of the filling station across the street from the Hardware Store. It was dark under the shed, but in the office a light burned. He got out and went up to the door. On the desk lay a man, suspenders down and his head on a rolled coat. There was an empty scabbard on his left hip.

"Hell, wake him up," Chicamaw said.

Bowie rattled the door and the man stirred, raised up and began to work his mouth like his jaws were sore. That old boy is a Law all right, Bowie thought.

Old Boy came out. He had a pistol in the scabbard now. "What do you boys want?" he said.

"Little gasoline, Pardner," T-Dub said.

Old Boy scratched his head. The hair looked like rope frazzle. "How much?"

"Fill it up," T-Dub said.

Old Boy moved toward the coupe; looked inside of it. T-Dub stepped toward him, brought the barrel of the revolver up into Old Boy's back like he was driving an uppercut. "Unlatch that pump, you nosy old belch before I beat your ears down good and proper."

Old Boy looked like he was trying to spit acid off the end of his tongue. Chicamaw snatched the six-shooter out of his scabbard. "And do it right now," T-Dub said.

"For God's sakes, boys," Old Boy said. "Take it easy now. I got a wife and four kids, boys. For God's sakes now. I'm an old man."

"You going to unlatch that pump?"

"For God's sakes, boys." Old Boy brought out the rattling ring of keys.

The car was serviced now and T-Dub told Old Boy to get in the car.

"We might just as well unlatch that hardware store over there while we're here and got him," Chicamaw said.

T-Dub drove with Old Boy sitting beside him;

Chicamaw and Bowie stood on the running boards. They stopped in front of the Hardware Store.

Chicamaw pried at the door with the tire tool and when the lock burst, it sounded like all four tires on the coupe had blown out.

Bowie pushed back the glass door of the gun-case and began piling the weapons in his arms like sticks of wood. Chicamaw was filling the cotton sack with shells and cartridges.

The town was still undisturbed as they left it.

Behind the high signboard, twenty miles from the town, Chicamaw bound Old Boy, pulling his arms behind a post and twisting wire around the thumbs.

"You can holler somebody down in the morning," Bowie said.

"That's all right, boys. Perfectly all right. You boys are all right."

The white center line of the black asphalt was running under them again like a spout of gray water.

"I'll swear," Chicamaw said. He was looking at the six-shooter he had taken off Old Boy. It was an old frontier model, a .38 on a .45 frame. "I wish you could see this."

"What is it?" T-Dub said. "Hell, I'm driving."

There were six notches on the cedar butt of the revolver.

"I didn't know we were doing business with a bad man," T-Dub said.

"Nigger killer," Chicamaw said. "That's how he got these on here. That town was full of niggers back there."

"I ought to have stuffed it down his throat," T-Dub said. "I got fed up on him right now. Started big-eyeing this car."

"He was trying to pull a smartie all right," Bowie said.

"That back there might heat us up a little," T-Dub said. "This car here now, but I believe these cotton sacks cover it pretty well. He never saw no license on this car you can tell the world. We got to get some duplicate plates though pretty soon. You can buy all them you want for a dollar apiece. We ought to get a dozen sets."

"Naw, that old boy back there couldn't tell you whether this was a truck or a Packard," Bowie said. "Squawking the way he was."

Day began to break with a haze like cigarette smoke in a closed room and the barbed wire and cedar posts of the fences and the low, twisted mesquite trees began to take form.   Bowie rubbed the bristle on his chin.   "You know I haven't washed my teeth since we left Alky," he said.

.   .   .   .   .

The wildcat-well spot was a good place to hole up for a day or so all right.   It was three miles from the Zelton Highway, a gully-scarred mesquite-clumped distance.   The weed-grown road beside it was as rough as a cog wheel.   It went on North, T-Dub said, beyond those cedar-timbered hills yonder and connected with a lateral road that tied up with the Gusherton Highway.

The mesquites were thick and made a fence for the clearing on which the old derrick rose.   Its timbers were as gray as an old mop; away from it a little piece lay a huge wooden bullwheel with rusty bolts.

Not even possum hunters ever came to this spot, T-Dub had said.   He had holed up here three days once after he sacked a bank.

This afternoon, the second that T-Dub had been away from them, Bowie sat on a spread cotton-picking sack, trying the action again of his .12-gauge pump gun.   He and Chicamaw had drawn straws for this Baby.   It had a pistol grip and a ventilated rib. But the rib was coming off and about four inches of the barrel just as soon as Bowie got hold of a hack saw.

Near the edge of the sack lay more of the guns they had gotten in the Hardware Store, the polished stocks and barrels glittering in the afternoon sun. There were two .12-gauge shotguns, a .30-30 rifle and a .30-06. There was a .22 pump rifle.

Chicamaw patted the scarred stock of the shotgun he had sawed off at Dee's. "I'll still take old Betsy," he said. "All you have to do with her is point her in a general direction." He was drinking. He had found a half-gallon of whisky in the back of the coupe that Dee Mobley must have left.

"This baby here has got a trigger pull and action like a watch," Bowie said. He brought the gun to his shoulder and drew bead on the pulley at the top of the derrick. "Boy, oh boy," he said. "What I could do to a covey of quail."

Chicamaw picked up the fruit jar and started unscrewing the cap. He extended it toward Bowie.

"I'll pass this time."

Chicamaw drank and then shuddered and clenched his teeth.

"Now when I get a pistol on me I'll be willing to call it a deal," Bowie said. "There's an army store in Gusherton, T-Dub said, and I might be able to pick me up one there."

"We got us enough guns now to start us a little war all right," Chicamaw said.

Bowie squinted down the sights of the gun.

"I'll take a .30-30 myself," Chicamaw said. "I can cut capers with them little gentlemen. I know one thing though you can shoot a man through the pratt with one and it won't bring him down. I saw it happen. I did it. Me and a couple of boys were running out of Wichita and a carload of Laws jumped us. That old wreck we were in wouldn't do forty. So I just told these boys to let me out at that bridge and I'd stop them gentlemen.

"I got out and here they come. I cracked down and them Laws started flushing out of that car like it was going to explode. One of them weighed around two hundred pounds easy and I popped him while he was running across a field. He just kept going. He didn't drop until he got in the timber."

"He finally dropped though, uh?"

"He told me about it himself later. He come up to Alky. He knew who did it. Laughed about it. Thanked me for not killing him. I could have killed him all right."

"I don't care about being jumped myself," Bowie said. "I'd just as soon they stay away from me."

"The Laws never got me in a rank but twice in my life. The first time was in this State and I was just a snotty-nose punk. I'd been unlatching so many safes that I'll swear I begin to think it was on the level."

Bowie laughed.

"They got me all right in this State once. Four years I done down here on one of these prison farms, boy."

"Man, I hear they're tough. These prison farms?"

"You heard right." Chicamaw started taking the cap off the jar again. "It's not everybody that beats them farms."

Bowie placed the shotgun on the ground and picked up the .22 rifle. "I always wanted one of these little guns when I was a kid," he said.

"That time they got me in Florida," Chicamaw said, "and sent me back to Oklahoma was just my fault. That landlady I was going with and me just got a little reckless. I wish I knew where that woman was. She wasn't no spring chicken, but I'll take her to anything you could ever show me."

"How come them to ever get you down there?"

"I had a run-in with a Jew down there in a gambling place. I was drunk. I don't mind telling you. This Jew didn't want to play stud poker. He had to play draw or nothing. I called him a Christ-killer and a few other things and he said he wasn't going to take it. I told him he'd take it or else. He started out of that place and I decided I'd better frisk him. I caught him and throwed down on him. He didn't have a gun on though. I was smart enough to get out myself because you know they're hard on you in that State for showing a gun, but I got too smart and went back there the next Sunday and there was more Laws on me than I thought there was in Miami."

"A man sure ought to stay sober Out Here," Bowie said.

"What are you trying to do, preach to me?"

" 'Course not, Chicamaw."

Chicamaw took another drink.

"There I was down there in Florida with twelve thousand dollars and a woman that was the stuff. That woman just wouldn't leave that town with me. Where I wanted to go with that stake was Mexico. Hole up down there like I did after beating them here in this State. If she had just gone with me."

"How is that Mexico business?" Bowie said.

"I done a year down there. It's just like any place else though. If you haven't got no money it's no good."

"I don't imagine I'd like it down there. Some of them greasers might try to kick you around like fellows do them up here and I wouldn't stand for that."

"If you got the pesos to throw, you can get by down there. But you can't make no money down there and when my four hundred dollars went I had to get out."

"I don't savvy their lingo either and gettin' across that border would bother me."

"I never had to show a passport all the time I was down there and besides, you can buy one. Fifty pesos will get you anything you want in that Chili country. Them Laws down there are all hoss thieves."

"You savvy that lingo of theirs?"

"Seguro."

"Rattle me off something."

"En Mexico hay muchas señoritas con culas muy bonitas," Chicamaw said.

"You're another one. What did you say?"

"I said there was a lot of pretty gals in that country with prettier behinds."

"You look kind of like a Spick anyway. That's

64

why you got by so good and then rattling off that stuff that way."

Chicamaw drank again. "I stayed on an old hacienda down there that was run by an old boy that used to be a thief himself. One of them revolution thieves. There was three more white guys on the place, all of us cooling off for something up here. I told you about Old Windy Hawkins."

"Who were the other two?"

"Banker from New Mexico and then the one we called Tangle Eyes. He was a deputy sheriff right out this line here close to El Paso."

"What did he do?"

"Killed a couple of farm boys. He just wasn't smart enough to make it. You remember when they had them big placards plastered up all over this state offering five thousand dollars reward for dead bank bandits?"

"Man, I was in Alky so long that I never knew nothing 'bout Out Here."

"They were doing it all right. This Tangle Eyes just planted a couple of old boys in front of a bank and let them have it. He just wasn't foxy enough."

"They don't still have that five-thousand dollar stuff in this State, do they?"

65

"Christ, no. The bankers had to stop it before they got everybody killed. The Laws were planting more people than there was bank robbers."

Spilled liquor wet the lines in Chicamaw's face, ran over his Adam's apple and down his neck. He put the bottle down and wiped his face on his shoulder. "You're in a good tough state, Boy. You didn't see that in the paper the other day. 'Bout five men dropping dead from heat prostration on that Bingham Prison farm. Heat, my hind foot. I know what killed them."

"I'm backing out of this just as soon as I get a little salted away," Bowie said. "I been intending to tell you boys."

Chicamaw lifted his left arm demonstratively and held his right hand up. "It's pretty tough when a man will take a hatchet and whack his arm off like this!"

"Goddamn, do they do that?"

"I saw four boys chop themselves in one week. One would whack the other and then that one would come down on the other one."

Bowie felt like his eyes were wired together.

"Them boys wanted to get off that farm pretty bad to do that, didn't they? And they just didn't want to get out of work. That's what they tell you in the Capital and them prison bosses say. There ain't a man in this State prison system that couldn't do the work they got. It's the way they work you and what they do to you."

"It don't sound good to me."

"Say it's cotton-picking time. All right. Maybe the cotton is five miles from the bunk house. Well, the building tenders rout you out at daybreak. Them are the little snitches that are doing a couple of years for busting a two-bit grocery and they give them saps and dirks and let them run over you. Anyway, they get you out and then the next thing you are going out in that field. Don't think you walk that five miles. You run it. Just as fast as that farm boss wants to lope his horse. And you do that back and forth three times a day. And if you fall out, it's spurs then and the bat or a barrel that night."

"That sure don't sound good to me."

"I've had them drop by me and they were as dead as doornails. And one of them Bosses sitting up there on a horse with a double-barreled shotgun and he can't even read or write and saying: 'Old Thing, ain't you going to get up?' "

"Man," Bowie said.

"Yeah, they call you Old Thing.   And if they get it in for you, you're not going to last.   They'll say 'Reach down there, Old Thing, and pick up that piece of grass.'   If you're not foxy and don't see that shotgun laying there in that grass, your pratt is mud because they want to go back and say you were trying to get to a gun."

"That sure don't sound worth a damn to me."

"I've heard that farm sound like a slaughter pen. Men squealing and begging like hogs.   You don't last on that farm if you're any man at all.   Unless you beat it.   Then you either come off there a whining rat or still a man."

"I couldn't stand them doing me that way," Bowie said.

The dreggy contents of the fruit jar jostled as Chicamaw shook it around.   He drank.

"No, I couldn't take that kind of stuff at all," Bowie said.

"Boy, I'm going up this road a long ways," Chicamaw said.   "Plenty of people are going to know it. I ain't going to kill nobody.   They're just going to kill themselves."

Bowie watched Chicamaw drain the jar.   Now I know why he ain't got no toes on that right foot, he thought.

68

Chapter V

THEY had a furnished house in Zelton now all right, but they were as broke as bums. In MacMasters yesterday too, T-Dub had almost had a rumble and then he came over here and almost the same thing happened. While he was getting the coupe gassed up in MacMasters, a car of Laws drove right up alongside of him with guns sticking out all over. It just turned out that the Laws were looking for a couple of fellows that had made a Hole in the jail in the next town. Then in this town he draws up at a *Stop* sign and right there, looking him straight in the face, is a Law he has known since he was a kid. But that Law must not have recognized him.

"Naw, he didn't recognize you," Bowie said. He was lying on the cretonne-covered iron cot of the living-room. "You could have told it the way he acted right there."

"It's not anything to feel good about anyway," T-Dub said.

"We got a good Hole-up in this joint though," Bowie said.

"Seventy-five dollars is a lot of money for a dump like this," Chicamaw said. He sat slumped in the rocking-chair by the empty fireplace. His eyes were red-veined from yesterday's drinking.

"Things are always high in these oil towns," Bowie said. "This is a pretty good place when you take everything into consideration."

It was a five-room corner house, three blocks off Main Street. On the corner back of them was a machine shop, grinding day and night. Across the street was a fenced-in lot piled with drilling materials. On the opposite corner was a church tabernacle and across from it a two-story, barn-looking building that was a lodging house for oil-field workers. Moving cars kept sand and dust sifting through the window screens all the time and there was nearly always somebody walking on the street.

Right now, the three of them were waiting on Mattie, T-Dub's sister-in-law. She had gone up to the hamburger stand on the corner to get sandwiches and a milk bottle full of hot coffee. She was using her own money to feed them.

"I'm fed up on running around in these overalls

like a damned Hoosier too," T-Dub said. "Now, Bowie, you look more like an oil-field guy in them khaki pants."

"I feel more like a hungry man than anything else," Bowie said.

"Quit crying, T-Dub," Chicamaw said. "I can get us some eatin' money from Old Windy over in MacMasters. I can give Mattie a note and it will be good for fifty bucks."

"Fifty dollars won't do us no good," T-Dub said. "It's going to take a couple of thousand. I'll be dog-goned if I'm going to charge this bank here half-cocked. We need cars and a bunch of stuff."

"It takes money to make money all right," Bowie said.

"You know that little town we come through this morning," T-Dub said. "Morehead? The one that's got the band-stand in the middle of the street?"

"Yeah," Bowie said.

"There's a bank there that I robbed when I was a kid. Sawed me off a bar and crawled through and got fourteen dollars in pennies. I used to live in that little town."

Bowie grinned.

"What are you grinning about?" T-Dub said.

"You crawling through them bars and sacking up them pennies."

"I was a cutter then. I was getting me some bicycle money. It was the day after Christmas."

"What were you saying about Morehead?" Chicamaw said.

"I've got half a mind to charge that bank there. I just got a hunch. That bank will go for four or five thousand."

"And it might go for five hundred," Chicamaw said. "I swore one time that I never would fool with them two-bit banks again."

"Beggars can't be choosers. What do you think about it, Bowie?"

"Anything suits me. Whatever you-all say."

"Don't get me wrong, T-Dub," Chicamaw said. "If you boys want to charge a filling station I'm with you."

"When you hear me talking about banks you're not listening to me talk about my first one," T-Dub said.

The footsteps on the porch were like a man's and they listened. It was Mattie though. T-Dub went to the door and she came in. She was a big woman with hips like sacks of oats; the lines in her face were like the veins in dried corn-blades. She had a grease-slotted sack in her hand. "I thought they never were going to get these damned things cooked," she said.

"What's the matter, Mattie?" T-Dub said.

"Nothing." She put the sack on the fireplace shelf. Her toes knotted the leather of the loose black pumps. "I'm going to be checking it to you boys though in just a few minutes. I got to get back to my job."

"I sure hate to see you having to work as hard as you do, Mattie," T-Dub said. "I sure don't know what we would have done without you."

Bowie nodded.

"This is a cash on the barrel-head proposition to me," Mattie said. "I need some money."

"You're going to get it, girl," T-Dub said.

After Mattie left they started eating the hamburgers and T-Dub told them about her. She worked in a sandwich shop for a dollar a day. Showed you what a woman would do when she liked a man. His brother had been in two years and she had never missed a week without sending him money. One woman in ten thousand. He was going to see to it that she got hold of a good piece of money so she could buy a lawyer and spring that bud of his. He was going to stake them to a tourist camp too. Wasn't going to be any more need of that brother of his having to be a thief.

"This is not getting that Morehead business settled," Chicamaw said.

"I'm just waiting on you two," T-Dub said. "We can sack them gentlemen up right tomorrow. Rabbit that seven miles through MacMasters and then cool off at that wildcat. When it gets dark, come right back through that town, right on over here and tomorrow night I don't think we'll be setting here quite as busted."

"Call your shot, Bowie," Chicamaw said.

"I'm in," Bowie said. "I'm ready."

"It's settled," T-Dub said.

Chicamaw said some boys liked to rob a bank before it opened and others around ten-thirty in the morning and two o'clock, but any old time suited him.

T-Dub said that the bank in Morehead didn't have more than three or four working in it and they wouldn't have to count on handling more than the same number of customers if any at all. This bank here in this town though would be a man-sized job.

Four men would be the best number to charge a bank like it. One man holding the car down outside and seeing to it that nobody came out; one holding down the lobby and keeping everybody in and the other two working the vault and cages and seeing to it that nobody kicked off any switches.

Bowie was lying on the cot again. I can rib myself up to do anything, he thought.

"Time you split money four ways though you haven't got enough to go around," Chicamaw said. "Three is plenty."

"I'm just telling you," T-Dub said. "These won't be the first banks I ever charged."

"I didn't mean anything," Chicamaw said.

"He didn't mean nothing," Bowie said. He sat up and looked at the hearth, but the cigarette stubs on it were too short to snipe.

"The Outside man has the hardest job," T-Dub said. "Some of these ding-bats think the guy in the car has the snap. But he's the man that gets the rumbles first. The Inside is a snap. I never saw a banker yet that wouldn't fork over as soon as you threw down on him. You can always figure that a man that's got sense enough to work in a bank has sense enough to act like a little man when you throw down on him."

"I've had to high-pressure a few of them," Chicamaw said.

"Only Hoosiers kill," T-Dub said.

"I don't believe you have to kill them," Bowie said.

"Them bankers will tell you to help yourself. It's insured. It's them billionaires up in New York that lose it. Them capitalists."

"I hope that Morehead bank will go for a nice piece," Bowie said.

"We'll get cigarette money anyway," Chicamaw said.

"Nossir, I've never robbed anybody in my life that couldn't afford to lose it," T-Dub said. "You couldn't hire me to rob a filling station or hamburger joint."

"I don't believe in that either," Bowie said. "Them boys in them filling stations don't make but two or three dollars a day and if they're robbed, they got to make it up. I'd just as soon beg as do that."

"I know one thing," Chicamaw said. "I'm going to be wearing me a fifteen-dollar Stetson and a sixty-dollar suit here pretty soon or it might be a black suit with some silk plush around me, but I'm sure not going to be wearing no overalls."

T-Dub went back to the kitchen and returned with three broom-straws. "The short man works the Outside," he said.

Bowie drew the short straw.

The others slept now. Bowie lay in the living-room's darkness, his elbow on the window-sill, his fingers scratching the screen. Five thousand, gentlemen, and I'm backing off.

The bed in the middle room creaked and Bowie listened. He smiled. That Indian, he thought.

Voices sounded in the yard outside and Bowie sat up, his hand extended toward the pump gun beside the cot. It was two men with dinner-pails cutting across the yard; going back to the machine-shop. Bowie lay back.

The next time I see that Little Soldier, he thought, I'll be driving a brand-new auto job and looking pretty good in a gray suit and red polka-dot tie and a flannel shirt with pearl buttons. I'll say to her: "I'm looking for that little girl that gave me a big lecture here a couple of years ago." She would look plenty surprised.   He'd get a smile out of her though.

Who was that snoring?   That old soldier.   I got to be doing a little of that myself. One . . . two . . . three . . . four . . . five . . . six. . . .

Chapter VI

WITH its four blocks of filling stations and lunch-
rooms on the north side of the widened highway and
then the intersecting, one-block main street, the
town of Morehead had a business district shaped
like a funnel. The funnel's mouth was corroded
with low buildings of stone and wooden fronts.
With Bowie driving the coupe, the three moved up
it now toward the frame band-stand at the end of the
block. It was ten-thirty o'clock.

The Farmers State Bank stood on the left corner
near the band-stand. It was a one-story structure
with two cement columns and barred windows.
"There's our meat," Chicamaw said. T-Dub
touched his forehead in a mock salute. "We'll be in
to see you in a few minutes, gentlemen. Don't be
impatient."

Bowie made a U turn around the band-stand and
then drove, motor idling, past the bank, the Pressing
Shop with its window display of bolted goods, the
patent-medicine display of the Drug Store and then

cut in to park diagonally in front of the Variety Store. In the Variety Store windows were women's underwear. To the left of it was a Meat Market and then a Grocery. Two farmer-looking men sat on cakes of salt lick in front of the Grocery. A youth in a red sweater with an M on it came out of the Pressing Shop and got in a truck.

T-Dub and then Chicamaw got out of the coupe. Chicamaw turned around, winked. "Ten dollars, the Sox beat the Giants this afternoon?" he said.

Bowie grinned. "Called."

The two moved up the street, the bagging seat of T-Dub's overalls wrinkling and Chicamaw's head bobbing on his long neck. They turned and entered the bank.

The bubble in Bowie's stomach broke and sprayed; he put the car in reverse, backed out and then moved down the street toward the highway.

The woman in the sedan ahead stopped parallel in front of the Post Office and Bowie turned out and passed her. That's the way I'll be parking in front of that bank in a minute, he thought. There were two men in broad-brimmed hats and boots standing on the corner in front of the Dry Goods Store. They did not look up. A dog, its ribs bulging, trotted across the street in front of Bowie toward the depot. There was a crated plow on the station's loading platform.

Bowie turned the second corner, passing the Lumber Yard. One block this way now and then another turn and he would be at the Bank again. That dream again last night? His Dad. He could hardly remember what his Dad looked like and yet he was as clear as himself in these dreams. Always the same thing happening. Him in that pool hall with his Dad and that other man getting ready to hit his Dad with the cue; him hollering and his Dad not hearing; him trying to shoot the gun and kill the man and the pistol breaking into pieces in his hand.

Bowie turned the last corner. Maybe that dream meant bad luck coming? If he counted to *thirteen* now with his fingers crossed, it would break the bad luck. *One . . . two . . . three . . . four. . . .*

Bowie stopped in front of the bank . . . twelve . . . *thirteen* . . . pulled the sawed-off shotgun up a little higher between his knees. Come on, Pals. Come on, you Old Soldier. Come on, you Indian. We got tall tracks to make. . . .

There were two more men standing now in front of the Grocery, one smoking a pipe with a curved stem. The pipe-smoker turned and looked up the street toward the Bank. All right, Square-John, that's a good way to get your eyes full and get in trouble. The man turned back.

T-Dub came out of the bank, the front of his over-alls bulging! Chicamaw following, two cigar-boxes under his left arm. Bowie looked up and down the street, across to the other side. Nobody big-eying or smelling anything yet.

They got in the car and Bowie gunned the motor; Chicamaw slammed the door. The two men sitting on the salt cakes stood up and the others turned and looked.

Bowie swerved onto the highway, the left wheels groaning; the approaching oil truck stopped with a jerk. The driver shouted. Bowie pressed the accel-erator harder; the *City Limits* dropped behind. The boy driving a cow with a stick turned his head and watched them go by.

"Anything behind us yet?" Bowie said.

"Naw," Chicamaw said. "Them guys are not going to get out of that Vault for a half-hour. They don't know the Civil War is over yet back there in that town."

T-Dub looked back. "Clear as a whistle."

"You-all do any good?" Bowie said.

"I think so," T-Dub said. He pulled a revolver from inside his overalls. "I picked me up a brand new Colt .45 here anyway. I'll will you that pearl-handled job, Bowie. Did you see me get it out of that till, Chicamaw?"

"Yeah, I saw you."

"Sacked up something else though, didn't you?" Bowie said.

"It went for three or four thousand, I think," T-Dub said.

Chicamaw turned back. "Naw, they don't know yet what it's all about back there."

A car zoomed over the rise ahead, hurtled toward them. It had a California license.

"Four thousand isn't bad, is it?" Bowie said.

"I don't say we got that much," T-Dub said.

"Man, you didn't expect us to stop and count it before we come out of there, did you?" Chicamaw said.

Bowie laughed.

The skyline of Zelton showed now: the fourteen-story hotel, the standpipe, the college buildings on the hill. "We're going to be holed up before they get out of that vault," T-Dub said. "Makes me half decide to go on to the house, but I want to save that place. We'll just go on to that wildcat."

Bowie turned the coupe off the highway and onto a dirt road this side of Zelton. They passed the Filteration Plant, the City Mule Barns, and then Bowie turned back East and presently they were on a paved, residential street. They crossed the town and cut back onto the highway by the Airport.

As they neared the turn-in to the old oil derrick, a car ahead of them approached and Bowie slowed. It was a big sedan with a negro driving and a man in the back seat smoking a cigar. After it was out of sight, Bowie turned the coupe onto the derrick road.

Chicamaw climbed the ladder of the derrick and started a lookout toward the highway. Bowie spread the big cotton-picking sack on the ground and T-Dub dumped the contents of the small canvas bag on it. The pile of currency, in rubber-banded packs of hundreds and twenties and tens and fives and ones, was as big as the crown of a cowboy Stetson. The two cigar boxes were spilling silver.

Chicamaw whistled and they looked up. "What's that stuff you boys are playing with down there?" he said.

"For Christ's sake," T-Dub said.

"Nose-wipin' paper, you damned Indian," Bowie said. "And there's ten bucks of it you'll never see. Them Giants have the Sox in a hole by now."

"Another ten says you're a liar."

"Accepted."

"Voices carry out here," T-Dub said. "You guys do your talking after while."

"Let's pipe down, Chicamaw," Bowie said.

T-Dub took four hundred and twenty-five dollars from the pile and snapped a rubber band around it. This represented the amount he had started out with and he put it in his shirt pocket. Bowie took a ten-dollar bill. "I'll take out six for Chicamaw," he said. "That's what he had."

Three piles of currency grew as T-Dub dealt out the bills like playing cards. Finally, it was divided and there was one thousand and twenty-five dollars apiece. The silver, it was decided, would just be left in the boxes and they would use it for general expenses like gasoline and beer and cigarettes. There were three or four hundred dollars of it.

Chicamaw descended the ladder and joined them.

"I just started telling Bowie here about that old banker back there," T-Dub said. "That old boy

like to have never got it in his head that it was a
stick-up."

"Never did put up his hands, did he?" Chicamaw
said.

T-Dub laughed. "He never did. He was sitting
at a desk there, Bowie, when we went in, just peck-
ing away at an old Oliver typewriter and I had to
almost kick the chair out from under him. 'What-
thehell?' he says. 'Whatdoyouthinkthisis?' I had to
yank him up and knee him back into the Vault. I
think we had the place half sacked before he ever
caught on."

"All them others acted like little men," Chicamaw
said. "They couldn't get in that Vault quick
enough."

"No customers?" Bowie said.

"One," T-Dub said. "Didn't you take a sack off
him, Chicamaw?"

"Yeah," said Chicamaw. "I got thirty or forty
dollars here I think." He pulled a small money sack
out of his hip pocket. "Naw, I don't have no kick
coming about that little Bank, but we could have
sacked up that Bank in Zelton just as easy. And had
ten or twelve apiece. Isn't that right, T-Dub?"

"We'll get to them gentlemen," T-Dub said.

Long ranges of clouds, thick as beaten egg-whites, moved in the afternoon sky. Through the rifts, the dome was as clear as bluing water. The only sounds were the thrumming cars over on the highway and they would stop and listen to them pass. When they talked now, it was in quiet voices.

As soon as it got dark, it was decided, they would return to Zelton and then Bowie could take the coupe out to the edge of the town and burn it. Chicamaw would get a bus and go to El Paso and come back in a couple of days with two fast, light cars and some extra license plates. T-Dub would go over to MacMasters, get Mattie to rent a car and they would get at least two more houses. One in Gusherton and one in Clear Waters.

"We ought to have a sure-enough set-up here in two or three more days," Bowie said.

"Might be that kid sister of Mattie's will go along with me and her to get them houses," T-Dub said. "You know, boys, I hadn't seen that little old girl since she was in diapers. Cute as a bug now. I want you two to meet her."

"What I'd like to have right now is something to eat," Chicamaw said. "You guys realize we haven't eaten nothing since them hamburgers last night."

"Funny, I'm not hungry," Bowie said. "What I could take on is a good tailor-made cigarette."

"I remember the last time I was cooling off in the country like this we had us a radio and we were gettin' a ball game," T-Dub said. "Chicamaw, maybe you'd better get radios put on them cars. Sure help to pass away the time when you're out like this."

Chapter VII

BUNDLE-LADEN Zelton people jostled and tripped and cut around Bowie in this Saturday-night shopping spree. He was downtown tonight just to stay away from that furnished house. Three nights now he had stayed in it alone and it was getting on his nerves. He had stayed in all morning and afternoon thinking that surely the boys would show up today, but Chicamaw was still somewhere out toward El Paso and T-Dub was rustling houses.

Tonight, Bowie had planned on going to a picture show, but there was nothing on at the two theaters except shoot-em-up cowboy stuff. Rain on that kind of show, he thought.

In front of the Drug Store with the window display of kodaks and photographs he paused now. There was a picture of a young couple with a baby; a hunter standing beside a car on the running board of which was an antlered deer; a bathing-suit girl in a canoe. Bowie peered closer. The gun in the hunter's hand was a .415 Winchester and the deer had six points.

Bowie went on. That Keechie Mobley would make a good picture, I'll bet.

Shaded lights behind the plate glass flushed the colors of the women's things; the silk blouses, dresses, hose, underthings. Now in a little town like she had to live in, Keechie never saw a bunch of pretty things like this.

In the panel mirror of the Department Store entryway, Bowie looked at his reflection: the iron-gray suit, the broad-brimmed hat, the white hand-kerchief in his breast pocket. His right hip pocket bulged a little with the .38 T-Dub had given him. Just as soon as I get around to it, I'm going to get a holster and strap and wear it under my arm. Then I won't notice it any more than my hat. I look pretty good though. What was it old T-Dub said about him: "That Bowie looks more like a Law than he does a thief." And Chicamaw: "Like a country boy come to town." That Indian.

Bowie turned and went back up the street, past the 5 & 10, J. C. Penny's, and on the corner, The Guaranty State Bank. He turned it and then was on Front Street, a dim-lighted thoroughfare of small cafés and dollar-hotels. On the other side of the street was the Texas & Pacific Railroad lawn with its mulberry trees, the depot and the freight offices and platforms.

A negro in a porter's cap and white jacket sat on a stool in front of the hotel doorway. On the white globe above his head were the lighted letters: *Okeh Rooms*.

"Looking for a nice lady friend tonight, Boss?" the porter said.

"Hell no, you black bastard," Bowie said.

In front of the *New York Café,* on the corner, a policeman stood talking to a bareheaded man who had one foot on the bumper of an automobile at the curb. Bowie walked past them. You got the advantage of Laws all right. You can tell them, but they can't tell you. And the detectives and deputy sheriffs out here might just as well have uniforms, you can tell them so easy. All of them in cowboy boots and white hats and black suits and shoe-string ties. And say that flatfoot back there recognized him when he went past? All right, all that Law had was a pistol. And didn't he have one on too? One thing though, he had to get out in the country pretty soon and practise up with this .38. Get used to it.

Bowie turned toward the railroad lawn, going to the furnished house.

There were two new-looking automobiles in the driveway of the house and Bowie checked the impulse to break into a lope. That Indian is back just as sure as the dickens, he thought. The cars were Ford V-8's. One a black job with a trunk and the other was gun-metal colored, both sedans.

It was T-Dub who let Bowie in. He had on a new blue-serge suit and tan shoes.

"Chicamaw come in?" Bowie said.

T-Dub thumbed toward the sound of rushing water in the bathroom. "Taking a bath and gettin' drunk as a Lord. I think he bought up all the tequilla in Juarez."

"I begin to think you two had fell in somewhere," Bowie said. "How long you been here?"

"I got here a little after dark and he was here then." T-Dub went over and lay down on the cot. There was a pile of scattered newspapers beside it.

"I guess you read about Morehead," Bowie said. "Wasn't that a joke? Got one number right in that license. *Three*. And calling it a green coupe and the only thing green about that old Chevvy was the stripe around it."

"Them newspapers never get nothing right. You been casing this bank here any?"

"Every morning since you-all been gone. I went down yesterday morning before daybreak and I been inside of it three times. That Vault kicks off either at nine or maybe before because it's open when the doors open."

"Who goes in first?"

"Nigger. The porter. Around six o'clock. It's a bird's-nest on the ground to go in with him. And the nearest Law is up at the Depot right at that time watching that passenger come in."

"Don't sound half bad."

"How you been doing, T-Dub?"

"We got them houses all right. She went with us on both trips. Lula. That's Mattie's kid sister. I told you about her though."

"Gusherton and Clear Waters?"

"Yep. That Clear Waters place looks like a millionaire's dump. Lula sure liked it."

"Them cars out there look like old Chicamaw has been doing his stuff. That was a job to tow that gun-metal job all the way in here."

T-Dub sat up. "You know I'd just as soon charge this bank here Monday as not. What do you say?"

"Tomorrow would suit me if it wasn't Sunday."

"I'm going to see the girls tomorrow," T-Dub said.

Chicamaw came out of the bathroom and into the living-room. He had on silk shorts and undershirt and his hair dripped water. The big veins of his biceps and forearms looked like pale earthworms.

"If it's not the old Country Boy himself?" he said.

"Hi, Chicamaw."

"Been teaching Sunday-school over in that tabernacle while we were gone?"

"I been asking for a job down at this nice little bank they got in this town."

"Old Bowie," Chicamaw said. "Believe anything anybody tells him." He looked at T-Dub and winked.

"Anybody except you," Bowie said.

Chicamaw laughed and his bare feet slapped the floor back toward the bedroom.

T-Dub picked up the newspaper again and Bowie went over and sat down in the rocker and lit a cigarette.

The flung newspaper rattled on the pile. "Every time I pick up a paper I see that damned little Squirt's name," T-Dub said. "If I ever run across him you going to see a guy get the damnedest behind-kicking a man ever got."

"Who's that, T-Dub?"

"Newspaper guy. He gave me the dirty end of the stick one time. I tried to make a Hole in this prison in this State one time and it went haywire and this Squirt comes to me and wants me to tell him all about it so he can write a big story for the magazine. Couple of the boys had gotten killed and I was shot right through the fleshy part here of my hip and it was all a mess. Everybody knew all about it anyway and this Squirt said if I would tell him the straight of it he would get it printed and split the money with me. I didn't even have cigarette money so I told him. You should have seen the way it come out in that magazine. I was the Big Shot, see. And I sent them two boys over that got killed first because I figured the guards would use up all their ammunition and then me and the other boy still down at the bottom of the ladder would have a clear way. Anybody knows that the Chair boys get the first break and that's why they went over first. Hell, I didn't go on up because the damned ladder had broke. One of them joint ladders you know. Then that Squirt getting it put in the magazine like that."

"Don't guess he ever sent you any money?"

T-Dub looked up and sneered.

Chicamaw came back in with a bottle of tequilla in his hand. He had on brown tweed trousers with pleats, a blue shirt and yellow tie. He offered the bottle and Bowie shook his head.

"For Christ's sake, come on and be human," he said.

Bowie took a drink.

"I ran into a pooloo in a sandwich stand close to Pecos that we knew up in Alky," Chicamaw said. "You guys remember that kid we called Satchel Pratt?"

Bowie and T-Dub nodded.

"He knew me right off and crawled all over that car and got to telling me how he knew where there was a good piece of money."

"Tin safe somewhere with thirty dollars in it," T-Dub said.

"I played him along. Told him I'd shove on and be back to the number he gave me right after dark and we would go and get together on that job he had."

"I remember that kid," Bowie said. "He played a banjo pretty good."

"I brought you something, boy from the city," Chicamaw said. "I run into some good Colt .45's out there and you can throw that .38 job of yours away."

"Man, I'm glad to hear that."

"You got to promise me that you won't sleep with it under your pillow though."

"Now what's the joke?" Bowie said.

Chicamaw looked at T-Dub and winked. "All right," he said and pointed his finger at Bowie. "I'll bet that's the way you been sleeping at nights?"

"Yes."

Chicamaw looked at T-Dub and then back at Bowie. "That's just what I thought. Look here, man. Always sleep with your gun under the cover by your side. Then if anybody walks in on you, you got as much of a throw-down on them as they got on you. Just let 'em have it. But you sure can't do any reaching up and behind you . . . like *this*."

"I never thought of that before," Bowie said. "I'm sure glad you told me, Chicamaw."

T-Dub stood up. "What do you say we start talking about this bank here? Bowie is ready to go Monday, Chicamaw."

"You don't have to ask me if I'm ready. I'm always ready." He lifted the bottle and there was a gurgling sound.

"Boys, it's going to be my thirtieth," T-Dub said.

Chapter VIII

LAST night, T-Dub had drawn the short straw, but because he knew more about the Inside of a bank, it was decided Chicamaw would drive the black V-8 and Bowie would go Inside with T-Dub. They had gotten out of bed at four o'clock this morning, driven out to the Derrick Hole and left the gun-metal sedan. Now it was six o'clock and they sat parked in front of the Sears, Roebuck Company store next to the Guaranty State Bank. The empty street looked as wide as a river.

"If Bowie and me are not out of there by nine o'clock," T-Dub said, "you better be coming in after us, Chicamaw."

Chicamaw lifted his head in a laughing gesture.

Somewhere the sound of a street-sweeping machine whirred and threshed. Away down the street, in front of the Café, a man came out and got in a car. The slamming door echoed in the canyon of buildings. The car vanished.

"Here it comes, Boys," Bowie said. He pointed

up the street. A negro in a gray rope sweater was approaching. Bowie and T-Dub got out of the car and stood beside it.

The negro was a middle-aged man with sideburns like steel wool. He stood there at the bank door, selecting a key on the ring. He inserted the key and grasped the knob.

"We're going in with you, Shine," T-Dub said. Bowie pressed the gun's barrel firmly against the rope sweater and they went into the bank's clean, early-morning gloom. Bowie squatted down and looked under the slit of the drawn blind. Chicamaw was driving off.

The negro breathed like he had been running, his wrists sticking rigidly out of the frayed sweater cuffs. "I doesn't quite understand this," he said.

"Don't bother yourself, Shine," T-Dub said. "You're liable to wake up with somebody patting you in the face with a spade if you do."

Bowie started tying the negro's thumbs behind him with copper wire. "Mistah, I been porterin' heah fawh twenty yeahs. You can ask anybody in Zelton. Everybody heah knows old Ted. Right heah in this bank fawh twenty yeahs. When they had the old building. Yassah, I been . . ."

"That's enough, Shine," T-Dub said. "Now you'd like to be able to go to church again next Sunday, wouldn't you?"

"Yassah."

"Then you just answer the questions I'm going to ask you."

"Yassah. I never lied to nobody in mah life. You can ask anybody in Zelton about me."

The clock over the front door indicated *6:30*. On both sides of the gray tile floor at the front of the bank were brown railings and inside of these were clean desks with lettered stands: *President . . . Vice-President . . . Vice-President. . . .* The bronze cages fenced the passageway of glass-topped tables back to the Vault. It was a big, broad door of aluminum and black colors. To the right was a passageway that led to the side-entrance door.

"What time does that big vault back there unlatch, Shine?" T-Dub said.

"Cap'n, that something I doesn't know about. Some the big bosses don't even know that. Mistah Berger knows about it."

"What time does he come down?"

"He's the fust one. Li'l' before eight."

Bowie moved around. Through the slits of the

Venetian blind at the side-entrance door he saw the closed, steel doors of the freight depot. An oil truck went past.

The clock clicked: *7:00*.

More automobiles were sounding on the streets outside now. A switch engine whistled and then the intersection railroad signal began to dong. The exhaust of a bus popped, fluttered. Bowie read the hand-lettered football schedule on the wire stand by the front door.

The knob of the front door turned and the man smelling of hair tonic and shaving lotion came in. He was short and had a belly as round as the sides of a mare in foal.

"Mister Berger?" T-Dub said. He had an open pocket knife in his left hand.

The man stood there, his left hand extended in a paralyzed, door-closing movement. His head went up and down.

"Mister Berger, this is a stick-up, and if you want to stay a healthy man, and I think you do, you'll just co-operate."

"I see," Mister Berger said.

It was *7:15*.

The heavy doors of the freight depot creaked and

groaned in opening. Box-cars bumped in the rail-road yards. Automobile horns sounded.

7:45.

Through the blind slots of the side door, Bowie saw the black flannel coat, the silk-clad ankles of a woman. He turned and T-Dub, standing in front of the Vault with Mister Berger and Shine, nodded. Bowie opened the door.

The woman gasped like she had been pricked with a pin and Bowie put his hand over her mouth. She became limp in his arms. "Take it easy now, Lady," Bowie said. "Nobody is going to hurt you."

"Be calm, Miss Biggerstaff," Mister Berger said, "these men are not desperadoes."

"I never kill anybody," T-Dub said, "if they just do what I tell them to."

8:30.

Bowie peered through the blind slots. The black V-8 was parked there now, Chicamaw's head down over a spread newspaper on the steering wheel. A match worked in his mouth. That Indian.

Mister Berger and T-Dub were inside the Vault now. A cage door clicked and rattled. Bowie's toes squirmed in his shoes. Sack it, T-Dub. Dump it in. Just a minute, Chicamaw. . . .

Mister Berger came out; then T-Dub with the bulging laundry sack slung across his back.

"Ready?" T-Dub said.

"Ready," Bowie said.

"We're going to take you folks with us," T-Dub said. "There's a Ford just out that door there and you go out there and get in it and don't let me see any of you looking at anybody 'cause if you do you're liable to get somebody killed."

There were two men in striped overalls working on the loading platform across the street, but they did not stop. Mister Berger and Miss Biggerstaff and Shine got in the back; then Bowie. He told Shine to lay on the floor. T-Dub got in front with Chicamaw.

They moved off. The young fellow parking the coupe stared. He had on a tan suit and horn-rimmed glasses.

T-Dub turned around. "You know him?"

"One of the boys in the bank," Mister Berger said.

The speed indicator rose: past the Candy Factory . . . Produce Company . . . Cotton Compress . . . Nigger Town. . . . A farmer, high up on the cotton wagon, saluted. Chicamaw waved back.

They crossed the railroad tracks and then sped up

the straight, dirt road toward the picket of telephone poles that marked the highway.

Miss Biggerstaff looked at Bowie. "What are you going to do with us?"

"Don't worry, Lady."

"I have done everything in the world I could, Men," Mister Berger said.

T-Dub turned around. "You folks just sit steady now. You have done all right and everything is okeh now."

Bowie could see the grinning lines on Chicamaw's cheek. He smiled too. The speedometer needle vibrated on *80*. Miss Biggerstaff shivered as if she were cold.

Holding to the top rung of the derrick ladder, Bowie saw the car leave the highway, its aluminum glittering like signal mirrors, and come onto this road. He whistled and below, T-Dub and Chicamaw picked up the corners of the spread cotton-picking sack with its piles of currency.

But the car was only turning around. Bowie whistled again and shook his head violently. The canvas was spread again.

Over in the black sedan, Mister Berger, Miss Biggerstaff and Shine sat, the feet of the men bound in copper wire. For three hours now, T-Dub had been dealing the bills and still he was wetting his fingers and going on. That's the prettiest sight I ever saw, Bowie thought. Bar none. He shifted his arm through the rung and grasped his belt. Bar none.

Chicamaw relieved Bowie on the lookout.

T-Dub grinned as Bowie approached. "Nossir, Bowie, that wasn't my first bank, but I never saw one go sweeter."

"I never saw a prettier sight then looking down here from up there," Bowie said.

Over in the black car, the glass rattled and Bowie saw Miss Biggerstaff rapping. "Go see what they want," T-Dub said.

Bowie came back. "It's the Lady. I think she wants to go to the bathroom. I think that's what she wants."

"She won't rabbit. Let her out."

"That Berger over there told me we got ten thousand dollars in securities here that's not worth anything to us and mean a lot to him."

"He's a damned liar. There's sixty thousand dollars' worth here, but he can have them back. They're no good to us."

At last the money was counted and divided. There was twenty-two thousand six hundred and seventy-five dollars apiece.

In the dusk, Chicamaw and Bowie tied Mister Berger and Shine to mesquites. Then Chicamaw went on up the road, out of sight, and presently they heard the motor of the gun-metal firing. It moved toward the hills and the Gusherton Highway.

Bowie drove the black car and T-Dub sat in the back with Miss Biggerstaff. "We're just going to take you up here a couple of miles, Lady," T-Dub said, "and then you can walk back and untie that gentleman friend of yours."

On the Gusherton Highway, Bowie and T-Dub got in the gun-metal with Chicamaw and left the flaming black car behind.

.   .   .   .   .

The house in the resort town of Clear Waters was an eight-room Spanish stucco with a patio, a three-car garage and big, sparrow-filled poplar trees in the parkways. It was a corner place and across from it was a four-story apartment house.

Bowie sat in the living-room now, soaking in its richness. There was a radio and a secretary and brocaded coverings on the divan and chairs. The lights on the rough plaster of the walls were shaped like candlesticks. Confession and Movie magazines littered the floor and the ashtrays were full of cigarette butts stained with lipstick. From the kitchen, where Mattie and Lula and T-Dub were cooking, came the smell of ham and eggs.

Chicamaw came in, his hair plastered and smelling of perfumed oil and indicated the room with a roll of his head. "Pretty good for some old boys that didn't have a pot or a window to throw it out three weeks ago, eh, Big Boy?"

"Pretty nice," Bowie said.

"You tied up with some fast company, didn't you, Boy?"

"I'll say."

Lula came in with T-Dub following. She was tall and had on a cotton house-dress and blue anklets. Her shaved legs had scratches on them and there was the tattoo of a red heart on the back of her left hand.

"Don't you think Lula and me would make a team," T-Dub said. They sat on the divan and T-Dub put his arm around her waist and began fingering the cloth over her stomach. "Last time I saw this little outfit she was just about up to my knees and now look at her."

"He's nuts," Lula said.

"I think you got him going, Lula," Bowie said.

Lula slapped T-Dub's hand away and reached in his coat pocket and brought out a package of cigarettes. She extended them toward Bowie and then Chicamaw. They shook their heads.

T-Dub held a match for her. "Yessir, this little girl is going to put a tattoo on her for me pretty soon." He winked at Bowie and then Chicamaw. "And it ain't going to be on her hand."

The smoke gushed from Lula's nostrils and she flecked the cigarette toward the ashtray. "I wouldn't be so sure about that now, Mister," she said. "And if I'm going up to that drug store before our midnight supper, you better be giving me a few nickels and let me get started."

Mattie came in. She had a dish towel tied over the black silk dress like an apron. "You boys come and get it. Was that Lula leaving, T-Dub?"

"We ought to wait until she gets back 'fore we eat," T-Dub said.

"Come on," Mattie said.

Their knives and forks scraped and slashed the

eggs and ham. "I don't wonder that bud of mine isn't working his head off to get out with cooking like this, Mattie," T-Dub said.

"It's not cooking that's going to get him out," Mattie said.

Lula thrust the newspaper toward T-Dub. "It's all over the front page," she said. "All over it."

T-Dub pushed plates aside and spread the newspaper, and Chicamaw and Bowie bent over him.

ZELTON, Sept. 28—In one of the boldest bank hold-ups in West Texas history, three armed bandits this morning robbed the Guaranty State Bank here, kidnaped A. T. Berger, vice-president, his secretary, Miss Alma Biggerstaff, and escaped with what bank officials estimated at more than $100,000 in cash and securities.

Berger and Miss Biggerstaff with Ted Phillips, negro bank porter, also kidnaped by the trio, were picked up by passing motorists, 21 miles east of here at 8 o'clock tonight. Miss Biggerstaff was in a hysterical condition from the day of terror and imprisonment.

Working with the precision of master criminals, the robbers entered the bank before the doors opened this morning. Arriving bank employees, unable to get into the bank at 8 o'clock, sounded the alarm. William Pleasant, bank bookkeeper, saw a black, crowded sedan leave the bank's side entrance as he was getting ready to park, but did not realize its full significance until later.

Today's holdup followed within less than a week

the $3,000 robbery of the Farmers State Bank at More-
head, adjoining community. Local authorities believe
both crimes were committed by the same band.

One of the bandits, Police Chief Robert Blakely announced here tonight, has been positively identified as
an escaped Oklahoma convict.

"Oh, oh," T-Dub said. "They got me identified."

"I don't care which one they got identified,"
Chicamaw said, "they ain't going to have to guess
long to know who was with you."

The food in Bowie's stomach felt like it was ex-
panding.

A posse of more than two hundred police officers and
citizens combed the country around here throughout
the day in a fruitless search. At a called meeting this
morning of the Chamber of Commerce, directors au-
thorized the posting of a $100 reward for the capture,
dead or alive, of any member of the gang.

"Now what did we do, boys?" Chicamaw said.

L. E. Sellers, a farmer living four miles east of town,
reported that a loaded car passed him shortly after 8
o'clock this morning, traveling East at a high rate of
speed.

The bandits were described as being well-dressed men
around 30 years of age.

"If it had not been for the bravery of Mr. Berger,"
Miss Biggerstaff declared, "I am afraid we would not be

alive to tell our stories. They threatened our lives almost every minute. Mister Berger talked to them coolly."

The two bank robberies in this vicinity this past week mark the first time in four years that a bank has been robbed in this section. The last one was at Stoctor, 40 miles southwest of here, by the famous Trawler gang. Trawler was hanged by an enraged mob at Stocton last December after he killed a jailer in a desperate attempt to escape.

T-Dub pushed the newspaper aside. "Well, boys, that's the situation."

"They sure did put it all over the front page, didn't they?" Lula said.

"The next time, Sweetheart," T-Dub said, "you bring us some good news."

"Christ, let's finish eating," Chicamaw said.

Bowie lay on the ivory-inlaid bed, under the smooth sheet and silken comfort, in the feminine, mirror-paneled room where the perfume of powders and toilet waters still lingered. That blows me up, he thought. Yessir, that sure blows me up on going back to Alky.

Up in the living-room, Lula giggled and then there was T-Dub's rumbling laugh. The Mexican orchestra of the Border radio station was playing *La*

Golondrina, a background of guitars strumming plaintively.

Bowie moved and the .45 was cold against his naked thigh. Yessir, that sure blows me up. But what are you gripin' about, Man? You got twenty-two thousand dollars right under this bed.

Chapter IX

ON THE afternoon of their third day in the Clear Waters Stucco, Chicamaw became staggering drunk and bumped around the house, his shirt tail hanging, and demanding who in the hell had hid his tequilla. Mattie and Lula threatened to leave and T-Dub became white-faced. Bowie finally got Chicamaw into the back bedroom. "Come on now, Chicamaw," he said, "and sleep a while. It'll be good for you."

"I'm not sleepy," Chicamaw said. "I'm drunk. I don't mind telling you I'm drunk. They ain't but two things I like to do and that's love and drink and there ain't enough women here to go around so I'm drinking. What do you think I left Alky for?"

"Don't talk so loud, Chicamaw."

"What do you think I left Alky for? To drink chicory coffee and look at art magazines?"

"Take it easy now, Pal."

"All right, old boy, old boy, old boy."

"You're scaring them girls."

"Let old Battle Axe leave."

"Snap out of it, Chicamaw."

"Old Country Boy is telling me what to do. You're just a big old farm boy, Bowie, but goddamit, you got something and I don't mind telling you, I can't figure it out. Let's you and me shell out of this place, Bowie. Go up to Oklahoma. Let's get us a bus and go to Dallas and get us a Packard and throw us a good one. You're going to Oklahoma with me, aren't you, Pal?"

"We ought to cool off here a few more days. There's still some heat out there."

"You going to Oklahoma with me, aren't you, Pal?"

"We'll talk about that later. What you want to do now is get yourself some sleep. You got to snap out of it, man. That real estate man was in here this morning taking an inventory and he big-eyed around plenty and that man that come up to the front door and said he was a census taker might just be nosying. There might be a little war around this place before you know it."

"You going to Oklahoma with me, aren't you, Pal?"

116

"We'll talk about that after you sleep a while. That and going to Mexico."

"Come on now, Bowie, wouldn't you like to go up to Oklahoma and see that little cousin of mine?"

"She's not interested in seeing me."

"That home town of mine is just forty miles from there and I want to see my folks, Bowie. I got to see them."

"I'd like to see Dee get three or four hundred dollars."

Chicamaw compressed his lips and closed his eyes and there was a whistling in his nostrils as he breathed. Bowie watched him for a little while and then bent down to unlace his shoe. Chicamaw's eyes opened. "You know why I want to go to Oklahoma?"

"Sure, boy. See your Old Man and Old Lady. And you want me to go along and stand on the corner with that pump gun of mine and see to it that nobody comes nosying around."

"That ain't all."

"You want to say hello to your folks."

"My folks know what I want and I got to take them the money to do it with. Them folks of mine haven't got a pot or a window to throw it out and I got to get them some money. Bowie, they ain't going to catch me floating around in no tank in them doctor schools if they ever get me. That's what they do to you if you can't pay the undertaker. They'll throw you in one of them tanks and carve on you."

"You must be drunk, boy, to talk that way."

"I want to be planted right. Goddamit, I'll give them every cent of it and I want to be planted right."

"I'll go get you a cold towel."

"Don't you leave me, boy."

T-Dub came in. His shaven face had a pink flush now and his hair was as white and soft as a baby's brush from the vinegar washing Lula had given it. He touched his forehead in a salute. "Feeling better, Chicamaw?"

"Who hid that tequilla, T-Dub?"

"Man, I don't know where it is."

"Tell that Battle Axe to rout it up."

"You're drunk, man, but you better start quieting down," T-Dub said.

"Old Foxy T-Dub," Chicamaw said. "Old Foxy."

Mattie came in, holding out a magazine. "Maybe this will sober him up some," she said.

It was a True Detective magazine and on the opened page were all their pictures: *Oklahoma Fugitives. $100 Reward.*

Bowie brushed it back. "He don't care about seeing that thing. Go burn that damned thing up."

T-Dub and Mattie left.

"Bowie, you going to Oklahoma with me?"

"If you'll go to sleep now I'll go. I don't mean that, boy. I'll go with you anyway."

"Then I'll go to Mexico with you, Bowie."

"That sure suits me."

Bowie lowered himself to the edge of the bed and after a little while, Chicamaw slept.

Bowie went up to the living-room and there were Mattie and Lula standing at the door, dressed up and bags around them. T-Dub was pale again. "The girls are going down to the Penitentiary to see my bud," he said. "I'm going to take them to the depot."

Bowie nodded.

"Your friend decided to quiet down?" Mattie said. The short fur jacket looked like she had another bag under it.

"He's all right," Bowie said.

"I was telling them that there's not a finer boy when he's sober," T-Dub said.

"He's all right," Bowie said.

"I hope we see you again soon, Bowie," Lula said. There was lipstick salve on her chin.

"Goodbye," Bowie said.

After T-Dub and the girls left, Bowie went back to the bedroom and looked at Chicamaw. He was snoring and had his mouth open. It was growing dark and Bowie stepped over and raised the blind a little. Then he sat down on the bench in front of the vanity.

I'll go on up there with him, he thought. There's nothing else for me to do and there's gettin' to be too many women around this joint. I'm ready to go to Mexico right now myself. If these boys want to rob that bank at Gusherton I'll help them, but I'm ready to clear out of this myself.

The breathing sounds in Chicamaw's throat sounded like air escaping from a flabby tire.

Mexico? Deer and wild turkey and cougars and bears even. A .414 Winchester would be the best for deer. A bear? Now that's something I'll have to do some figuring on when I get down there. Christ. If I was in Mexico with a .22 I would be satisfied. And just rabbits to hunt. Let me down there, man, and I'll run them rabbits down on foot.

The front door sounded and Bowie went up to

the living-room. It was T-Dub. He went over and sat down on the divan and began flecking at bits of cigarette ash on the blue serge of his broad thighs. "I hated to see that little girl go," he said.

"You'll see her again," Bowie said.

"That Chicamaw back there has got it down all wrong," T-Dub said. "You can't make women a money-on-the-barrel-head proposition. Love 'em and leave 'em. It don't work when you meet somebody decent. He's nuts though."

"This business is no good for a girl," Bowie said. "That's what he means."

"Where would we have been if it hadn't been for Mattie?"

"I know it. It's a proposition."

T-Dub said that if Bowie and Chicamaw went to Oklahoma, he might go down to Houston and try and get Lula to go off with him on a little trip to Galveston or New Orleans. Mattie would come back and keep their houses held down. He had given her two thousand dollars to buy a car and have something to run around on.

Bowie said he and Chicamaw would come in and do their part on that two thousand.

In the distance, a siren sounded and they looked

at each other and listened. The sound grew nearer and then they heard the bells of the fire engine clanging and they relaxed.

"But I been thinking, Bowie, and you're not going to get three together like us again nor a set-up like we got now. In a couple of months if we just stay foxy we can have fifty thousand apiece and then will be the time to back off for keeps."

"If we're going to charge that bank at Gusherton I'm in favor of doing it and gettin' it over with."

T-Dub shook his head. "These banks out here are looking for trouble now. Look at what happened to those two kids day before yesterday. Trying to work right in our heat."

"You kill somebody though like they did and your heat really gets hot."

"They were Hoosiers."

Bowie began cleaning his finger-nails with a split match.

"What I want to do," T-Dub said, "is get me about fifty thousand salted away and invest it in one of the Big Syndicates and get it paid back to me two or three hundred dollars a month. I'd like to find me a doctor that's a thief like us and get him to saw off these finger-prints and I'd grow a beard about a foot long and rear back up in them Kentucky hills on that little farm and let the mistletoe hang on my coat tail for the rest of the world."

"I hate to stay cooped up like this in a house," Bowie said. "I'm like a mule though, I never know what I do want."

"You got to put up with things I don't care how you make your money. And you take a chance in anything. Take them aviators. I got a cousin that's in the army and he was writing my bud and telling him how he was soloing around up there. I'll bet that kid don't last as long as I do."

"I know I'm in this a lot deeper than I planned to be. I'm going to be like that Indian back there I guess. Go up this road as long as I can. Win, lose or draw."

"I made my mistake when I was a kid," T-Dub said. He lifted his leg and looked at the polished toe of the shoe critically. "But a kid can't see things. I should have made a lawyer or run a store or run for office and robbed people with my brain instead of a gun. But I never was cut out to work for any two or three dollars a day and have to kiss some-body's behind to get that."

"I don't guess I could have done anything else

except what I have," Bowie said. "What will be, will be."

A little after midnight, Chicamaw's feet padded in the hallway and then he came into the lighted room, rubbing his nose and twisting his face. "Got a cigarette, anybody?" he said.

Bowie gave him a cigarette. Chicamaw went over and sat on the divan by T-Dub. The cigarette trembled in his hand and he began rubbing his ankles together and finally he reached down and scratched the left one. "What time is it gettin' to be?" he said.

"After twelve," Bowie said.

"What have I been doing around here?" Chicamaw said. "I feel like hell."

"You just been guzzling a little," T-Dub said. "The girls left."

"Did they?"

"They went down to see my bud."

Chicamaw scratched his other ankle and then his elbow.

"Bowie and me have been talking business," T-Dub said. "If you boys are going to Oklahoma, what do you say we let things rock for about a month and all of us meet up again in that house in Gusherton, say, November fifteenth?"

The cigarette fell out of Chicamaw's hand and he grunted as he picked it up. "Suits me."

"I'm in," Bowie said.

"November fifteenth in Gusherton then," T-Dub said. "Boys, if we sack them up over there it will be my thirty-first."

Chapter X

IT WAS cold this morning and the fallen leaves of the poplar-trees rustled and clattered on the sidewalk in the wind. Bowie carried Chicamaw's black Gladstone and his own brown strapped bag out to the gun-metal and put them in the back seat. In Dallas I'm going to buy myself an overcoat. Pretty good to know you got the old mazuma in your pockets to buy yourself a coat and anything else you might need. And I sure got it on me. Seven thousand in that bag; ten thousand in this coat pocket and these two pants pockets. And three thousand in silver in the trunk of this car.

Chicamaw came out with the guns in a blanket and then T-Dub with a black Gladstone. T-Dub's collar was turned up around his throat and he moved like his bones were on hinges. He said it was rheumatism.

"All you need is a good dose of Lula," Chicamaw said.

At the Sante Fe depot downtown, T-Dub got out,

saluted and grinned and went on in. He was going to Houston.

On the road to Dallas, Bowie and Chicamaw talked about how they were going to do things there. They would register in at the biggest hotel, Bowie as *A. J. Peabody* and Chicamaw as *Frank Masters,* baseball players from Denver, Colorado. They would stay there all day, Chicamaw getting his car, and right after dark take out for Oklahoma.

"You better not go too strong on one of those big cars," Bowie said. "Get one of them big jobs and everybody will be big-eyeing you."

"That shows you what you know about it, boy. If I could get me a green Packard with red wheels and a calliope whistle I'd do it. Then they big-eye the car instead of you."

"After we give this car to Dee I think I'll get me another V-8," Bowie said.

The quiet of the thick-carpeted hotel room—*814*—was that of a bathroom and Bowie, alone now, soaked in it. A hotel is just about the safest place for a man, he thought. Say one of these hotel clerks thought he saw something? Well, he wouldn't be in any too big a hurry to call a bunch of Laws in. People staying in hotels wouldn't appreciate a little war busting in their faces. Then it was pretty hard for a man to get in a rank as long as he was throwing money. People taking your money just didn't run off and squawk. Men just weren't made that way. He took a sheaf of currency from his inside coat pocket and dropped it on the blue counterpane. "And, Brother, I got it to throw."

After bathing and shaving, Bowie went down and sat in the lobby. Everybody around him had on pressed suits and shined shoes and watch chains across their vests. They're not the kind of fellows that big-eye you, Bowie thought. It's these Hoosiers in these little filling stations that don't have anything else to do but chew tobacco and look in them damned detective magazines.

After a little while, he went to the street and started looking in the shop windows. In a mirror he studied his hat and decided that the brim was too broad. Too much like a cowboy. He went in the Department Store on the corner, and besides the new hat he bought a double-breasted blue overcoat, two handbags and a powder-blue suit with a belted back. I'll show that Indian a fancy thing or two in duds myself.

In the Jewelry Store, he bought an open-faced

watch and chain and then a ladies' wrist watch with six diamonds on the band. That Little Soldier will open her eyes when I hand her this.

It was noon when he returned to *814* and Chicamaw had not showed up.

He tried on the powder-blue, but it was just too much of a go-to-hell suit for him. That Little Soldier would give him the laugh if he turned up in it. What am I ribbing myself up about that girl for? I'm just going to fool around here and make a donkey out of myself. That girl has other things to think about besides a damned thief like you, Man.

Now was the time, he decided, to send some money to Mama. Five of these one-hundred dollar bills with one of these pieces of hotel stationery around them and one of them envelopes. I wouldn't mind sending her five thousand if it wasn't for that no-good husband she's got. He'll get every damned bit of it. Now if it was that second husband she had it would be okeh. He was a pretty good fellow. Dumb, but I wouldn't mind helping him.

Old Jim and Red up there in Alky could sure stand a few bucks. Jim sure liked his sweet milk and them charging twenty cents a quart up there in that Prison when you could buy it in town for a nickel. And old Red wouldn't smoke nothing but tailor-mades. I'll get to you boys. I'll stop in one of these post-offices pretty soon and send you boys a hundred apiece. I've got to do some stopping in some of these towns pretty soon and get some of these dollar bills changed into twenties. Got enough of them things to pack a washtub. I'll just start shoving them through these bank windows, twenty and thirty at a time, and pretty soon I'll get rid of them.

Bowie pulled off his shoes and lay on the bed. *814.* Oh, oh. *Eight* plus *one* plus *four* equals *thirteen.* Aw, there's nothing to that. That's carrying it too far.

Mexico? Man, money will go a long ways down there. Three of them pesos for a dollar. Twenty thousand? Jesus Christ. That would be forty-five thousand pesos even after he took out for a car and the other expenses he would have while he stayed up here. Now if I go on through with it at Gusherton? Jesus Christ. I'll be a damned rich man. . . .

Bowie woke up with Chicamaw standing above him. "I thought I was going to have to pop my pistol to get you up. Man, you'd be a pushover." He smelled of liquor.

"What time is it?"

"If we're going to get out of here right after dark we better be gettin' in the saddle."

Bowie had the delicate, spraying feeling in his belly.

When Chicamaw, up there ahead of him in the new Auburn, held out his hand, Bowie slowed and then turned in to park alongside of him at the sandwich stand. It was a neon-lighted place with beer signs and a lettered board of sandwich prices. When the uniformed girl came out, Chicamaw said he wanted twelve bottles of beer to carry.

After the girl went back into the stand, Chicamaw pointed up the street toward the filling station on the left corner with the *Gas . . . 13¢* sign. "I run in that very station up there once and there was an old boy in there that sure big-eyed me. He had a wooden leg, I remember. I noticed him, see, out of the corner of my eye and finally he says to me: 'Boy, it ain't none of my business, but I know you.' I says to him: 'Brother, you just think you know me.' He says: 'You're Elmo Mobley as sure as hell, but after you leave here, I never have seen nobody that even looked like you.'"

"He really knew you, did he?"

"Sure he did. But I never did let on, see. He says to me: 'Boy, I just wish you had got this bank here 'fore it went busted and took my wad. I'd rather for a poor boy like you to have it than them god-damned bankers. Both of them bankers are out of prison now and still living swell on what they stole from me and about four or five hundred more folks here.' "

"I'll be doggoned. He was Real People."

"I gave him a ten and told him to keep the change."

"You run into Real People once in a while all right."

The girl returned with the bottles of beer in a sack and Chicamaw put them in his car. He said to Bowie: "If you're in such a big hurry, I'll just let you set the pace out of this town and I'm telling you, boy, you better stomp it or I'm liable to run over you."

"Okeh," Bowie said.

Bowie moved out the boulevard toward the Oklahoma Highway, the rear-vision mirror of his car reflecting the following lights of Chicamaw's automobile. I'm going to be in Keota in an hour and a half. This buggy is going to get stomped. He felt of the small hard bulge in his left vest pocket. Yes, the watch was still there. He pressed the accelerator harder.

The one-lamped car approached on the intersecting street ahead from the right, but there was a Stop Sign there and Bowie stepped back on the gas. The other car lunged right on across the Stop Sign and Bowie stomped brake and clutch, swerved, but the One-Lamp hit and then a bucket was shoved down over Bowie's head and tons of shattering glass were burying him. He thought: *This is liable to get me in trouble. . . .*

Thrown from the sprung door of his car, Bowie rose from the parquet grass, feeling like the figure in a slow-motion picture. He was on his feet now, a terrific weight on his back. Yonder was his car, the radiator caved in against a broken lamp-post and behind it was an old coupe, somebody inside of it groaning, its one lamp still burning.

Human forms moved like shadows about Bowie now. "Are you hurt, Friend?" a Shadow said. "No," Bowie said. He moved toward his car, dragging the weight that was like a plow. I got to get that stuff. *. . . I got to get that stuff. . . .*

134

It was a woman in the wrecked coupe: "Oh, my God. Oh, my God. Oh, my God. . . ."

Bowie reached his car, grasped at the handle with hands that felt like they had gone to sleep. He staggered with the push. "Get on over in my car, you damned boob," Chicamaw said.

Somewhere now there was a sound like a thousand trucks straining up a high hill in first gear. Them's not trucks, Man, Bowie thought. Sirens. His fingers groped at the emptiness of his right hip. Gun gone. That's the kind of luck I have, gentlemen. He moved across the street, through the working Shadows, dragging the Plow, toward Chicamaw's car.

He climbed into the front seat and then thrown bags were thumping in the rear. To hell with the rest, Chicamaw, boy. Come on. Everybody and his dog is coming. . . .

The flashlight was like a blow-torch in Bowie's face. The Voice behind it said: "What's your hurry, Buddy?"

"I'm in no hurry," Bowie said.

"I'm taking him to a doctor, Officer," Chicamaw said. Another bag thumped in the back. "He's bunged up pretty bad."

"I'm pretty bad bunged up," Bowie said. The

135

flashlight clicked off and then he saw Officer, the bulging chin that was like a licked hog's knuckles. Another form in a black hat was with him.

"Where you from?" Officer said.

"Denver," Chicamaw said. "You fellows come on to the hospital, by God, if you want to ask questions."

"There's a woman over there hurt and from what I can hear you were traveling too fast," Officer said. "You get out of that car and come on with me. And you too, Buddy."

"Not this time, Friend," Chicamaw said.

Second Officer said: "Listen here, Bub, you going to get in jail yourself here 'fore you know it."

"Not this time, Friend. . . ." Shoes scraped and then the hoofs of a thousand horses were thundering on a tin roof above Bowie's head. Guns! Bowie reached toward the panel pocket: *This is liable to get me killed.*

Like a cut radio, the noise ended. Then Chicamaw was getting under the wheel; the motor roared like an airplane taking off and Shadows scattered in the street ahead of them like cotton-tail rabbits.

The car sliced the highway wind with the sound of simmering water. Chicamaw pressed the panel button and the illuminated speedometer, to Bowie, glowed through a mist. Chicamaw tapped and the instrument board was dark again. "You're bleeding like a stuck pig," he said.

"I'm all right."

"You better snap out of it."

"It was a Little War."

"They were men enough to start it. Let 'em be men enough to take it."

"It was an old one-light Jalope that got me. Come right out and got me good."

"I'm going to dump you at Dee's. There's plenty of heat behind us and I'm going to let you out and get on up the road and burn this car."

"It was a Little War. That old Jalope."

"You're not hurt bad, are you? You're bleeding like a stuck pig."

"I'm all right."

They whipped around the red tail-light of another car; then the twin glow of another.

I'm just sick at my stomach, Bowie thought. That's all. Why I used to get sick just from standing up when Mama was cuttin' my hair. Her name was Peabody then. No, that was the first man. It was Vines, the carpenter one, then. See, Chicamaw, that shows you I have snapped and my mind is clear. Vines was his name. Pain seized Bowie's back with the grip of a twisted monkey-wrench and his belly muscles became as rigid as a washboard.

"What the hell?" Chicamaw said.

"I'm all right."

Chicamaw ran the car under the darkened shed of Dee Mobley's filling station, got out and vanished behind it. Just let me lay down for an hour, Bowie thought, and then I'll feel just as good as ever.

Chicamaw came back with Dee and when Bowie got out, his legs felt like cooked macaroni and he sunk to his knees. "Ain't that funny?" he said. They carried him back to the Bunk.

"I put everything under the bed here," Chicamaw said.

"Thanks, Chicamaw," Bowie said.

The motor of Chicamaw's car roared and he was gone and then Dee Mobley gave Bowie a drink of whisky. It clawed his mouth and throat like finger-nails.

Dee kept sitting down and getting up and moving around the room. Finally, he said: "You're not hurt bad, are you?"

"No," Bowie said.

"You see any use of me staying here?"

Bowie shook his head. "Not a bit, Dee."

"I don't know what kind of trouble you boys got in," Dee said, "but I don't see any use of me hanging around your heat. You're welcome to this place though, and if it wasn't for the fact that I'd be losing money I'd just as soon close it up and put a sign out there on the front door and go up to Tulsy. I could put plenty of grub in here and water and you could stay here as long as you wanted."

"Don't worry about the money."

"I got to worry about it, Bowie."

Bowie gave Dee ten fifty-dollar bills. "You better let your folks know to stay away from here."

"Nobody comes around here except Keechie and I'll give her some of this money and she can visit up in Muskogee or somewhere."

"You better do that."

The scraping branches of the pecan-tree against the Bunk's tin roof sounded like cat claws on a screen. I could be a lot worse off, Bowie, old boy, and don't you think different. I could be laying back yonder. You doggone whistling. I still got the money. The silver is gone, but to hell with that. That old Jalope. *814*. That was it. *Eight* plus *one* plus *four* equals *thirteen*. There you are; that was it. And if it hadn't been for that Chicamaw?

Chapter XI

DAWN oozed through the cracks of the closed Bunk door, the veins of the drawn window-blind, and pressed with leaden heaviness on Bowie's frozen soreness. The suit of winter underwear, Dee Mobley's, hung on the post of the bed like a scab. I will get up in a minute, Bowie thought, and light that stove. I'm chilled and that's what is wrong with me.

He touched his loosened front teeth with his tongue and heard them creak in their sockets. A car droned around the curve, thundered past the filling station and faded with the sound of a covey of quail in flight.

I'm going to get up. *One for the money, two for the show.* Now when I say *four to go,* I will get up. But what's the use of gettin' up? I've got all day. *One for the money* . . . Chicamaw won't be gone more than two days. He might show up right to-night. *One for the money* . . .

This might not really be happening, him lying here in this place and getting ready to get up. This was just his Spirit? His Real Self was back up that road. No, that was his Spirit too. His Real Self had got the Chair. I'm like a cat with nine lives. That's it. One of them in the Chair and one of them back yonder. Seven left. I'm going to go ding-batty if I keep lying here. *One for the money!* . . . A car was coming under the shed of this filling station. Bowie sat up, his right hand reaching for the floor. Man, you don't even have a gun. . . .

The knob turned and then the unarmed figure in the red sweater was standing there. It was Keechie. Bowie's face felt like it was encased in a cellophane mask and if he breathed his skin would crackle.

She closed the door and came toward him. "What's the matter with you?"

He breathed. "Accident."

She stood beside the bed. "What's the matter?"

He touched his mouth. "I guess you see my lips now. They're busted up pretty bad."

"Anything broke?"

He shook his head.

"Shot?"

"Just sprung my back a little."

She went over to the kerosene stove and then a match popped and the igniting wick sputtered.

Bowie lowered himself back to the pillow. The pan of water rattled on top of the heater.

Two lines creased Keechie's face from her cheekbones to the corners of her thin, dry lips. Her eyes were the color of powdered burnt sugar. "Hungry?" she said.

He shook his head. "Your Dad said you were going up to Muskogee or some place."

"Uh huh."

"I guess he left all right."

"Yes."

"I guess you better be careful about staying here, Keechie. I've been in a little trouble."

"You look like it."

The hot, wet towel melted the brittle casing on his face, softened his lips. Her fingers touched his face and he wanted to lick them. Just let her stay a little while. Just a little while. . . .

"I got money," he said. "On me and in that brown bag under this bed. Nineteen thousand dollars."

She straightened, cupping the towel in her hands, looked at him.

"I don't know why I said that."

"I'm glad you have it if that's what you want."

"That wasn't what I wanted to say. What I wanted to say was I don't guess it's best for you to be here."

"You need help."

"I just thought that I had this money and maybe you would like to take a trip or go some place. All girls like to go places."

"I don't know what other girls like to do."

"Now I didn't mean anything by that, Keechie. Now don't get me down wrong."

"I would do this for a dog," Keechie said. "If you will turn over and pull your shirt up I will put some liniment on your back."

She left at noon, but she was coming back. It would be after dark and she would bring plasters and cigarettes and something for him to gargle. She would leave the model-T and walk back out, telling her Aunt Mara that she was leaving town. She would sleep in the filling station at nights.

Bowie rested on the bed, his back and head propped against a quilt and pillow. It's all right, he thought. I've had more than my share of bad luck and I know it's going to be all right for two or three days.

The cotton underwear on the bed looked like the skin of a dead rabbit. Bowie got up, picked the rusty file from the window sill and scraped the garment to the floor. Then he kicked it under the bed.

Chapter XII

THEIR spoons tinkled in the peanut-butter glasses of soft-boiled eggs and crumbled crackers. Keechie sat on the edge at the foot of the bed, the golden glow of the oil heater's jagged crown caressing her face.

"It's about time you started eatin' something," Bowie said. "I never heard of anybody not eatin' any more than you do and not gettin' any more sleep. Just two or three hours a night. I never heard of it."

"I've gone three nights without sleeping and it doesn't bother me at all. I've done it all my life."

"You've fallen off some too since I saw you last and you better start sleepin' and eatin' more, young lady. Now me, I've got to have my eight and nine and ten hours at night or I'm just blowed up."

Their spoons scraped in the emptied glasses and they laughed.

"Don't you ever want to leave this town, Keechie?" Bowie said.

"Yes." She got up and took the glass out of his hand; placed it with her own on the table. Then she came back and sat down. She talked. Her voice was as soft as the reflection on the heater's dull brass.

Once, she said, an old couple drove into the filling station and she got acquainted with them. The man was paralyzed and they were touring the country for his health. They dropped her post-cards and talked about her coming to live with them and she would like to have gone, but then the cards stopped and finally one day she got a card from the woman saying the old man was dead.

"It makes it pretty hard on a girl when she doesn't have . . ."

"Have what?"

"A Mama."

Keechie shook her head. "It depends on the mother."

"I don't know what I would have done without mine. Never has bawled me out for a thing."

"My Aunt says my Mother is the reason why my Father drinks and goes on like he does, but that doesn't have a thing to do with it. He is no good and perhaps she was, but I can't see that she is any better."

Outside, there was a sound like the sirens in

Texaco City and Bowie stiffened and the skin on his chin and throat stretched.

"What's the matter?" Keechie said. She got up.

It was only wind in the telephone wires over on the highway. "Nothing," Bowie said.

"Your back?"

He shook his head. "This old world is some old world, ain't it, Keechie?"

"Yes."

"Who's your fellow, Keechie?"

"Why do you ask that?"

"I just thought I would ask."

"Why?"

"It isn't any of my business. Most girls have fellows and I was just asking."

"I don't know what most girls have."

"I don't believe you like men folks, do you, Keechie?"

"They are as good as the women I have seen."

"I believe you are kinda down on people."

"I don't know."

"And you never have had a fellow?"

"No."

"Even just to go to church with or something like that?"

"No. Why, do you think I should have?"

"Why, no. I was just asking. That's your own business."

"I never did see any use of it." Keechie reached over him and picked up the pack of cigarettes on the window-sill. The breasts under the polo shirt stirred.

"I'll take one too," Bowie said. "You know I don't know what could have happened to that Chicamaw. I guess he is seeing his folks."

"You will get along a lot better if he stays away from you."

"Aw, Keechie, you just got that cousin of yours down wrong."

"I'm not kin to anybody."

"You're a Little Soldier, that's what you are."

"Why do you call me that?"

"Because you are.   Isn't it all right?"

"Yes."

She went over to the table and picked up the granite coffee pot and looked inside of it. She put it down and then picked it back up.

"Keechie."

She turned, the coffee pot in her hand.

"You know I have been wanting to give you something ever since I been here and I'd like to give it to you now."

"What is it?"

"A little old watch."

She returned the pot to the table.

"Do you want it?"

"Do you want to give it to me?"

"Yes."

"Yes, I want it."

Chapter XIII

ON THE fourth night, Chicamaw came, his eyes like a dog sick with distemper, his face the color of ham rind. Bowie's head quivered on his neck and he called, but Keechie left the Bunk without speaking to Chicamaw.

"You look like you been making it all right," Chicamaw said.

"I been all right."

"Well, I haven't been doing so well. I've throwed every cent I got."

"I'll swear, Chicamaw. What's been the trouble?"

Chicamaw said he had throwed it in a Tulsa hotel gambling. He did have a new car though and some guns. A tommy gun too. By god, he had a Big Papa out there now and he was as ready as anybody to start a Little War.

"You didn't see your folks?"

Chicamaw shook his head and began plucking at a hair in his nostril. "I didn't want to go around them as hot as I was, Bowie."

"Well, you're not broke, Chicamaw. I still got it, see, and you're welcome to what you need."

"Sure makes me anxious to get back with T-Dub in Gusherton and get me another piece of money. You going to feel like getting up in a few days and running these roads again?"

"I guess I could go right now."

"No, I wouldn't ask you to go now. If you'll let me have five thousand I'll go on over and see the folks. Make it six thousand. Will you do that?"

"Christ, yes, man."

"Can you beat me throwing that much though, Bowie? You know I'm a damned good poker player. They just took me to a cleaning. When I get to thinking about it, damned if I don't believe there was something crooked about it."

"Them big gamblers are thieves. You better stay away from them, boy."

"I guess you been reading the papers all right?"

"I haven't seen anything."

"Is that so?"

"I been just laying right here. You mean Texaco City?"

"Man, we're hot."

"Them Laws?"

"We're hotter than gun barrels, boy."

There was a scratching sound and Bowie looked toward the closed door expectantly, but it did not open. It was the pecan-tree touching the Bunk.

Chicamaw left the Bunk and returned quickly. Bowie had the brown bag on the bed and was taking money from it. Chicamaw put the two .45's on the bed.

"Sure glad to see them guns," Bowie said.

"Thanks for this loan," Chicamaw said. "You know I been thinking about you, Bowie. You don't throw your money away and you don't get drunk. You're just a big old country boy, Bowie, but by God, I believe you're going to make it. You got something and I just can't figure it out."

"It didn't do me no good in Texaco City."

"Well, I guess I'll be shoving off, Bowie. Now if I get jumped and can't get back here in a couple of days or you have to rabbit from here, I'll see you in Gusherton. We sure can't let old T-Dub down."

"You be careful, Chicamaw. Go a little easier on the whiss, boy."

"Then if I don't see you here in a couple of days I'll see you in Gusherton?"

"What is it them Mexicans say when it's okeh?" Bowie said.

" *'Sta bien,* " Chicamaw said.

" *'Sta bien,* " Bowie said. "Man, I sure do want to get down there in that chili country some of these days. A man can't live like this always, Chicamaw. You know that."

"We'll make it down there, boy. Don't you worry."

Chapter XIV

IN THE early mornings, when shadows crawled in a gray gloom and Bowie lay alone in the Bunk, he thought of First Officer, his hog-knuckle chin; the smothering bucket and shattering glass; the Chair, Spirits, Cats. The branches of the pecan-tree scratched the roof a hundred times and Keechie was never coming, he thought. For God's sake, man, *snap*. But at last she did come and then all that screwy Spirit stuff got out of his damned head.

In this evening's twilight, the polished peanut-butter glasses glowed with the delicacy of a blue flame. Bowie watched Keechie: the flipping cloth in her hands was like a blowing skirt and he seized her bare, strong fingers with his gaze. She had paint on her mouth tonight, but looking at her lips was like spying on her unclad through a keyhole.

She straightened the drying cloth on the back of the chair and then picked up the kerosene can. "I'd better fill up your heater for tonight," she said.

"You ought to put a coat on," he said.

While she was gone, he planned what he would do in the morning when he woke up. He would not read the Sunday newspaper she had gotten him until in the morning. And then he would only look at the funny pages and the comics.

Keechie returned and filling the stove, she came to the bed. "I hope you get a good night's rest."

He played with the point of his shirt collar. "I hate to see you go."

"Do you?"

"I guess I've kinda got the blues tonight."

"I have done about everything I could around here, but I'm in no hurry. If you want me to stay——"

"Just a little while if you ain't in no hurry."

She lowered herself to the edge of the bed and crossed her legs. The sound of the tree now was like a gentle rain.

"I don't like to look behind," he said. "I try to just think of maybe the good things that will happen ahead. But I guess I know what is going to happen."

"No, you don't, Bowie. The things that you are afraid of most never happen. I'm a lot older than you in a lot of ways."

"I never have seen nothing like you before,

Keechie. **I** know now what makes a fellow get him a little missus and swing a dinner pail."

"You mean that?"

"Yes."

She moved and he reached out and said: "Don't go."

"I'm not."

"My ears are ringing," he said.

She bent toward him and touched his face. He seized her then, brought her toward him. "Don't you go. Don't you go."

"I'm not, Bowie."

Strength swelled within him. I can snap her little body in my hands. I can break her little body in my grip. Her tight lips yielded until there was only softness and then her breath became as naked as her body. . . .

. . . . .

Frying bacon spluttered in the skillet on top of the oil heater and then it popped and Keechie jerked back and turned and smiled at Bowie.

"You better be careful, Little Girl," he said. She sure did look different. Where did he ever get the idea that she wasn't pretty? Those lines in her face.

Where were they? And that little mouth was as soft and pretty.

"Wonder if you could take time out and come over here and give your Daddy a kiss?" he said.

She came over, the fork in her hand and bent down. "There's nothing sick about you," she said.

He kissed her. "I feel like a million bucks. I been thinking about getting up and running a half-mile before I eat."

"You just stay there. How do you want your eggs?"

"Any old way."

"How do you want them?"

"Any old way, honey. Over easy I guess. And hand me that newspaper over there while you don't have anything else to do."

She handed him the newspaper and he pointed at the three pale prongs of sunlight that lay on the splintered floor near the window. "Look, I believe the sun is going to shine today."

"I noticed the stars last night and I thought then that it might be clear today."

He began turning the pages and then he saw the thing that seized his eyes like a fish-hook:

TEXACO CITY, Texas, Oct. 6—Fingerprints found on the steering wheel of the wrecked, new automobile which the fugitive slayers of Plainclothesmen Vic Redford and Jake Hadman abandoned here last week, may lead to the identity of the killers, Chief of Detectives Musser revealed here today. The chief said his department was basing its hopes on this and also a revolver found nearby.

Redford and Hadman, veteran peace officers, were ruthlessly slain in a gun battle on Ector Boulevard while investigating an automobile crash. A woman received minor injuries in the collision.

"Are you very hungry this morning?" Keechie said.

The white of the paper glimmered like heat on the highway and Bowie jerked his eyes away. "I didn't understand what you said?"

"What's the matter, Bowie?"

"Nothing. Not a thing. I was just reading here."

"What are you reading?"

"Just something here."

Six suspects arrested here in connection with the case have been released. Two are still being questioned.

The abandoned automobile of the killers was purchased in El Paso, Texas, it was reported. Witnesses of the battle say that three and possibly four men were in the car that sped away after the shooting. One witness declared he saw a woman in the outlaw machine.

A police benefit here last night for the widows of the two slain officers netted $320.

Bowie took the warm plate with its eggs and bacon from Keechie's hand and put it on his lap. After a little while, he stuck the fork into the egg's yellow.

"What's the matter, Bowie?" She sat on the bed's edge with a plate on her knees.

"I don't want to hold nothing back from you, Keechie. I'm pretty deep in this business. I'm a lot deeper in it than I was when I was here before. I want you to know that."

"What is it?"

"I had some trouble back up the road. Two Laws killed."

Keechie placed her plate on the floor.

"You can see that I'm in it pretty deep now."

"Did you do it?"

"Them Laws?"

"Yes."

Bowie's head went up and down.

"You did not. You can't tell me that. I know who did it. Chicamaw. You can't conceal anything from me." She clutched his trouser cuff. "He did it."

"It don't make any difference who did it. And

you got Chicamaw down all wrong. I wouldn't be sittin' here now if it wasn't for him."

"You did not do it, Bowie."

"I wouldn't tell you nothing but the straight. I got it on my back and there's no gettin' around it."

Keechie got up and the plate on the floor rattled and broke. She looked down at it and for a moment her mouth twisted as if she were going to cry.

Bowie held up his plate. "Don't mind that. We can split this."

Keechie picked up the plate fragments and the spilled food. On the table was Bowie's untouched food.

"I'll just tell you the straight of it, Keechie. I'm not sorry. I'm not sorry for anything I ever did in this world. That when I was just a punk kid and they put the Chair on me don't count. But I'm not sorry for a one of these banks. The only regret I got is that I didn't get one hundred thousand instead of ten. I'm just a black sheep and there's no gettin' around it."

"The only thing black about you is your hair," Keechie said.

"You're a Little Soldier, Keechie. You're a Little

Soldier from them toe-nails of yours up to your hair, but you can't get mixed up with me."

Keechie's face twisted like he had driven his fist into it. He grasped her arm. "Keechie, what's the matter?"

She shook her head.

He pulled her to him. "What's the matter, honey?"

"Didn't you mean that last night?"

"Mean what?"

"Bowie. You know what you said."

"Honey, I can't think of everything right now. What was it, honey? You come on now and tell me."

"You said you wished you had me."

"Sure I do. Godamighty, honey."

"What do you mean then? Getting too mixed up with you?"

"Don't you see how it is? When a man has them Laws after him and it's all in the papers they'll shoot you and ask questions afterwards. They'd just as soon shoot a woman down with him as not."

"Is that what you mean?"

"You see now, don't you, honey?"

"Does anybody else have any strings on you,

Bowie? Anybody else?" She pulled away from his grasp.

"What do you mean?"

"Is there anybody else? A woman?"

"Oh, no, honey. Lord, no."

"I just wanted to know."

"How come you to ask a thing like that?"

"I'm in this pretty deep and I just wanted to know."

Bowie lay back against the pillow. "Keechie, come and lie down beside me a little while."

She got on the bed beside him.

"You like me, Keechie?"

"Yes."

"A whole lot?"

"Yes."

"Hundred bushels full?"

"Yes."

"Thousand bushels full?"

"Yes."

"A hundred thousand million trillion gillion bushels full?"

"Yes."

"Keechie, I love you." Her finger nails dug into the flesh of his throat.

·   ·   ·   ·   ·

There were sounds in the filling station and Keechie got out of bed and went across the darkened room to the door; Bowie following, in his underwear, a .45 in his right hand. Keechie peered through the cautiously opened crack of the door. After a long time she closed the door easily and Bowie stepped back. "It's my Aunt. Stealing some groceries."

Neither was sleepy now. They lay in bed, both their heads on the one pillow. "You know I been thinking, Keechie. This business of me staying here can't go on. I been here eight days now and Dee is going to be coming back pretty soon and this just can't go on now."

"Do you have anything in mind?"

"How would you like to go somewhere with me?"

"You want me to go?"

"You know doggone well I want you to go."

"What do you have in mind?"

"I'd like to get in a big city, Keechie. I mean like New Orleans or Louisville. Old T-Dub was always talking about them towns. In them big cities, people don't big-eye you so much and if you keep your nose clean, you can last as long as you want to."

"I guess so."

"I just don't know what's happened to that Chica-maw. That Indian can take care of himself though. He's probably gettin' everything fixed up at his folks'."

"We don't have to go around any of them, do we? Mister Masefeld and them?"

"No sir, honey. Not you. I should say not."

"I've been thinking some too, Bowie, and what I have had on my mind is what some people that used to live next door to my Aunt told me. Mister Carpenter and his wife and they had a girl my age named Agnes. Mister Carpenter had tuberculosis and they moved away down in Texas almost to the border in the Guadaloupe Hills. Agnes wrote and told me about it. They lived away out in the hills and wouldn't go to town for two months at a time and Agnes said that the only people they ever saw were some Mexican sheepherders and then a few sick people like Mister Carpenter. People chasing the cure, Agnes said they were."

"Close to Mexico, uh?"

"Bowie, I don't see why we couldn't go to a place like that and just live to ourselves and pretty soon people would forget all about Bowie Bowers and then finally there would just be the real Bowie Bowers."

"You know I hadn't thought of that. Them little towns though, Keechie, are bad. Everybody wants to know your business."

"We won't be in a town. We'll be away out and don't have to see anybody."

"You know I sure hadn't thought of that."

"That's where I would like to go."

"Man, we got the money to do it. Right here under this bed and in my breeches and coat yonder."

"I think that would be the best and just stay away from everybody you ever knew."

"How you and me going to get out of this place, Keechie? No car or nothing?"

"We can manage."

"Any trains stop here at night?"

"Two o'clock to Tulsy."

"We could get that train, by golly. You could walk about a half-block ahead of me and get a couple of tickets and I'll be hanging around and every once in a while we'll give each other a wink and then we'll sit in separate seats on the train and . . ."

"We'll sit together on the train."

"Sure, we can sit together on the train and then

168

we'll get in Tulsy and I'll buy us a new V-8 and then we'll scat down to this Guadaloupe Hills country. Where is that place, Keechie?"

"I've looked at it on the map a hundred times. When Agnes was writing me I wanted to go down there. There's deer and wild turkey and squirrels and everything else, Agnes said."

"Man, I could knock me off a deer. I'll get me a .30-30 or a .415 Winchester and you and me will eat venison, kiddo. You just let me down there, Keechie, and I won't even need no gun. Just give me a rock."

"If we go down there, either you or me will suppose to be a lunger, you know, with t.b. Maybe both of us had better be. Now in renting a cabin or something we'll have to let on."

"I'll look like the best t.b. in the world."

"That's the thing for us to do. And you just forget everybody you ever knew."

"You'll have to get you some clothes in Tulsy, honey. How about a fur coat? To set that watch off I gave you?"

"We'll think about that later."

"I'll buy you a whole windowful of clothes. You

can get anything you want. All you got to do is name it."

"We can't look like no millionaires. We're going to be sick people."

"Ah, you can get a few things. How you like them riding boots and pants, Keechie? Aw, I don't know though whether I'd like to see you in pants or not. You just get dresses. And plenty of them silk doodads. We'll get a couple of thermos jugs and keep them filled with soda pop and get some blankets and sun glasses and an extra can or two of gasoline and we'll split the breeze."

"When do you think we should go?"

"What time is it now?"

"It must be twelve."

"We can make it. Two hours. Let's get in the saddle, honey."

"Tonight, Bowie?"

"You doggone whistling. And honey we got the money to do it on too. Twenty thousand good old bucks. I mean fourteen. That's a lot of money, Keechie. You can say what you want to about money, Keechie, but by god, it talks."

"I guess so," Keechie said. "Well, let's start dressing."

Chapter XV

MESQUITE trees persisted even into this foothills country, but the Plains were far behind now. There were Spanish oaks and cedars and in the late afternoon this way the sage grass had a lavender flush. Away ahead, in the distance, a long range of sharp hills embroidered the horizon. Above the range, the sky was streaked with white, rigid panels as if the rain had crystallized and awaited a crack of lightning to unleash.

Keechie was driving and Bowie sat low in the seat, his hands deep in his pockets. She drove like Chicamaw, her left hand on the cross-bar and the other on the wheel; took the curves like they weren't there. In the holster under Bowie's left arm was a .45 and in the panel pocket another. There were four blankets in the back, a thermos jug of coffee, a sack of sandwiches, four cartons of tailor-made cigarettes. And Keechie had on hose that cost two dollars and shoes that cost ten and that military cravenette coat. It was her own fault that she didn't get the fur, but she looked like a Little Soldier in that coat and he had to hand it to her. And the way she had that little brown hat cocked over her eye. . . .

Down the road, beyond the Curve sign, the cement disappeared around the stone-studded bank; straight ahead, low, white barriers and space and blue sky. What if they just kept going straight and into that space and sky? They would keep going like a plane right over that valley. But cars don't fly. What if they did go off? It would just mean that he and Keechie had drawn the poor cards. But what if they made it? It would mean Luck was riding with them for a long time to come. . . .

The wheels of the machine sung tenaciously on the curve and now they were on a long straight-away again. They ain't nothing going to stop us, Little Soldier.

"Light me a cigarette, Bowie."

"Yes, ma'am."

The dairy barn was white with green trimming and over its roof, white and black pigeons circled. On the porch of the house lay a big dog, its paws dangling over the edge. They passed an old sedan, its slender wheels wobbling, the top tattered and in pennants.

"Them old Jalopes," Bowie said. "They cause more accidents than anything else on the road. It's no crime to be poor, Keechie, but there ought to be a law against letting cars like that out on the highways."

They passed a Schoolhouse, two filling stations and on the porch of the General Store sat two men bent over a checker board. The black lettering on the highway board read: *San Antonio . . . 186.*

Down this highway, thirty miles more and then they would turn west on a dirt road. Out that road one hundred miles and they would be in them little hill towns, Antelope Center, Arbuckle. There they would start house hunting.

On the left was a cemetery with a half-dozen low tombstones and then an unpainted, box house. Farther down, at the wooden gate, two cows with swollen bags waited.

"You know anything about cows, Bowie. Do they ever have twins?"

"You got me there."

"I was just wondering."

"It looks like to me they could though. With that woman up in Canada doing what she did, it looks like to me a cow could do it."

"Those cows back there made me think of it."

"That woman up there in Canada, Keechie. That shows you nothing is impossible in this old world, doesn't it?"

"It sure does."

"And I was thinking back there. What is it you say we are doing? *Chasing the cure.* Well, what if we really did have t.b.? Well, I don't know but what I'd rather be a lot hotter than I am now than have something like that riding me. Don't you kind of feel that way about it?"

"I should say I do."

Bowie chose the big filling station with its stucco front and Keechie turned the car up the curving driveway. There was another car under the shed, a woman at the wheel, but it drove off as they stopped. The next time we gas up, Bowie thought, we'll be having us a home to go to. Just fifty miles more now and they would be in that town of Arbuckle.

The filling station attendant in the leather jacket said: "Yessir?"

"Fill 'er up and I got a couple of cans."

Keechie entered the Rest Room door and Bowie

went over to the Coca Cola box and lifted the lid. The exhausts of stopping motorcycles popped and he turned. The two cops were coming right in here.

The Cops came toward the Coca Cola box and Bowie moved over. The tall cop was as brown as saddle leather and the short one had chapped, scaling lips. They had on gray uniforms and black Sam Browne belts. Their pistols were pearl-handled.

"What kind you want?" Tall Cop said.

"Coke," Short Cop said.

Their lips made drinking sounds on the mouths of the bottles.

"Got you a new one there, haven't you?" Tall Cop said.

"Yeah," Bowie said. "Them jobs over there can outrun it in reverse though, can't they?"

"They'll outrun that car all right."

"I guess them motorcycles there will outrun just about anything that gets on these roads, won't they?"

"Don't you think it, Mister," Short Cop said. "There's plenty of them out there I don't go after."

"You can tie them up in traffic sometimes," Tall Cop said.

"Ninety is about all I want to push that 'cycle over there of mine," Short Cop said, "and if anybody has anything that will do better than that I just check it to them."

Keechie came around the corner, stopped and then started smoothing the dress about her hips. Bowie winked and she went on to the car and got under the wheel.

"That all, Sir?" the Attendant said.

Bowie paid him.

They drove off and Bowie turned and reached toward the back seat. Tall Cop and Short Cop were sitting on top of the Coca Cola box.

"You didn't bat an eye, you doggone little dickens. Not an eye."

"What were you talking to them about?"

"Damned if I know."

"It looked like to me you were trying to make friends."

"They didn't know me from Adam's off ox, Keechie. Why, they're that way all over the country. How they going to know you? Look at a picture. Well, what's that?"

"I would stay away from them."

"Man, when they drove in that station though, I says to myself: 'Here's where a Little War starts.'"

"You better look behind."

Bowie looked back. The ribbon was clean. "Not a thing, honey. Nossir, you didn't bat an eye."

"I think maybe I had better start carrying that pistol in the pocket there, Bowie."

"Not that big gun, honey. That thing would jump clean out of your hands. I'll get you a little gun one of these days pretty soon though. Every woman ought to have a gun. I'm going to get you one. There's always some sonofabitch ready to get smart with a woman."

"I'm not afraid of that gun."

"Did you ever shoot a .45?"

"No, but I have a real strong grip. I could out-crack any of the girls in school on pecans. You remember that game. I won all the time."

"Yeah, I remember that game. What did we call it?"

"Hully gull."

"That's it. Yessir, Keechie, it just goes to show you how a man don't have to jump from his shadow. I'll bet I could go right up to the Law over here in this town of Arbuckle and ask him if he knew of a furnished house and I'll bet he wouldn't know me from Adam's off ox."

"I will do the asking about the houses. I will go to the real estate office and do the asking."

"You going to tell them we're lungers, sure enough?"

"That is what we are down here for now, Bowie, and you want to remember it."

Bowie made a coughing sound and slapped his chest. "The bug is gettin' me down. How's it doing you, Little Lunger?"

"You'll make it, old Foot-in-the-Grave."

.   .   .   .   .

There were no furnished houses in the little town of Arbuckle or near it, the Real Estate Woman told Keechie, but over at Antelope Center, she said, forty miles farther West, the cottages of an old Sanitarium were being remodeled for tourists and sick people and deer hunters. Bowie and Keechie went to Antelope Center.

It was almost noon when they left the graveled highway, two miles west of Antelope Center, turned through an arched gate and started climbing the narrow, high-centered road. Through the cedars and frost-browned oaks, on the side of the Hill, stood a big gray building.

178

"Looks like a jail," Bowie said.

"It won't hurt to look," Keechie said.

The closed building was the old hospital, its cement the color of dead broomweed. Through the dust-filmed windows there were stacks of bare beds and piles of mattresses. Back of it and east, rows of small stucco cottages fenced it like a carpenter's trisquare. The cottages had glassed-in rooms and stone chimneys and there were lettered boards over the entrances: *Come Inn . . . Suits Us . . . Journey's Inn . . . Bella Vista.*

The man raking the weeds in front of the corner cottage in the V of the Square stopped, leaned on the handle and looked at their car. When Keechie got out, he dropped the rake and came toward them.

The man had on a khaki army shirt and a white cloth belt held his slick, blue serge trousers. He was middle-aged and his teeth were broken and tobacco-stained. Yes, he had some cottages. He was the caretaker out here. He had just fixed up another cottage and it was twelve dollars and fifty cents a month and that included water and electricity. It was the last house at that end. Now he lived in that house on the corner, and below him a School Teacher batched and next to him an Auto Salesman with his wife and two children. They were the only ones that lived out here now, but he hadn't got around to fixing up any more cottages. They were fine people, the folks that lived out here.

"You want to look at it, honey?" Keechie said.

"Yeah, I'd just as soon."

"You take that School Teacher feller yonder," the Caretaker said, "he got him a hot plate from Sears, Roebuck and he's just batching fine."

Bowie got out of the car.

The Caretaker thrust out his hand. "Lambert is my name, young man. Old Bill Lambert. Traveled out of San Antonio for thirty-five years, leather goods, saddles, grips and harness. Had a lung collapse on me here a year ago and this air up here, Son, is fine. What's your business, Son?"

Bowie removed his hand from the other's grip. "I'm a sick man right now. Used to play ball."

"Son, you come to the right place. Not a healthier place in the United States than right in here. Ball Player, uh? Well, we got a School Teacher and two Salesmen and now we got a Ball Player. Now that Salesman feller over yonder used to be worth a right smart of money. Owned his own business right yonder in Antelope and just went busted like any of us can do. His wife didn't like it much out here at first, her being used to gas and fancy things, but now she just likes it fine. Your missus will like it too."

"Pretty quiet out here, I guess?" Bowie said.

"You won't get lonesome. Now that Salesman has got him a radio and everybody out here is fine people."

"Used to be a lot of people out here, I guess?"

"I don't know all the history of this place. Now all this was built right after the War, I think, and then it petered out and then for a while it was a sort of tourist camp and I might just as well tell you folks because I'm not the kind to hold nothing back. This place got a pretty bad reputation with the folks in Antelope because here a couple of years back some bootleggers got out and people come out here and throwed wild parties. But that's not any more, son. Your wife will be just as safe here as any place in the world now."

"He has to stay awful quiet," Keechie said. "Let's go look at the place."

Bill Lambert walked ahead on the narrow sidewalk in front of the closed cottages, talking, spitting. "Now it's nothing swell, you know, but I'll fix it up just like you want it. There's one thing, I want to put you in some linoleum in the kitchen and if you ever have company and need an extra cot, why just let me know."

He stopped in front of the last cottage—*Welcome Inn*—and opened the scraping screen and inserted the key in the lock. The wooden floors inside creaked under their feet. In this front room there were a blackened, empty stone fireplace and an iron army cot covered with a yellowed counterpane. There were two hide-bottomed rocking-chairs and a rickety breakfast table. In the windowed sleeping-room there was a broad iron bed, a huge dresser with a smoky mirror and two straight dining-room chairs. The kitchen had a three-burner, grease-caked oil stove, a sink and an enamel-topped table. The bath had a shower and the toilet seat was split and part of it lay on the cement floor.

"Some strong lye soap and a mop and whitewash would help a lot around here," Keechie said. "Don't you think so, honey?"

Bowie grinned. "Don't you think the price though will about keep us busted?"

"Now I tell you, Mister . . ." Bill Lambert said, "What did you say your name was, Son?"

"Vines. V-i-n-e-s."

"Well, I tell you now, Mister Vines. It's just the best I can do. A bunch of millionaires own this out here and you know how they are. I been trying my best to fix these places up here and get some money to do it with because people just want things a little nicer for the money, but I tell you, it's just like gettin' blood out of a turnip to get something from one of these millionaires. Now you take Mister Philpott over there, he's the Salesman, they've fixed that place up over there just as pretty as a picture."

"There is a lot to do around here all right," Keechie said.

"I'll tell you what I'll do," Bill Lambert said. "I don't want to rush you folks, but if you decide to take it I'll throw in a half-cord of wood for nothing and tack that linoleum down the first thing this afternoon right after dinner."

"We must stay awfully quiet," Keechie said.

"Don't you worry about that, Mizzis Vines. Now you take here last month, it was the night of September fifteenth, there was a couple come out here and I thought I smelled liquor, but I didn't want to cause no trouble and I let them have the place although they just wanted it for two or three days. Well, before the night was over she was running around right in this house here, without anything on and kicking up as high as them trees and the blinds up to the ceiling and so I just politely told them we didn't want that going on around here. Now, Son, you want your wife protected and that is just the way I do out here. This is a place for respectable people and any time anybody runs around here kicking . . ."

"That's all right, Mister Lambert," Bowie said.

"Just one more thing now, Mister Vines, and then I'll let you go. Now you take Mizzis Philpott over there. One day she goes off and while she's gone her oil stove burns over and I busts in there and saves the whole place. They were mighty appreciative of that."

"I'm very satisfied," Bowie said.

"If we ever catch you in this house, you had better be putting out a fire," Keechie said.

Lambert laughed. "All right, Lady. All right. Now then I'll just leave you two together and let you decide."

Alone, Bowie and Keechie walked in the rooms. "Think it will do, Keechie?"

"I'm crazy about it."

"If I ever catch old Filthy MacNasty peepin'

184

around here, I'll kick his hind-end clear off," Bowie said.

"He's harmless. Bowie, this is just the thing."

Bowie walked in the sleeping-room, Keechie following. "Some of them big, red Indian blankets would sure look pretty in here," he said. "And we'll get us a big radio to sit in yonder."

"I can go to town this afternoon and I'll buy enough groceries to last us three months," Keechie said.

"I forgot to ask old Filthy if there was really some deer around here," Bowie said.

Keechie sat on the edge of the bed and moved up and down on it experimentally. "Good springs and mattress, Bowie."

"I'm sold on it myself," Bowie said. "Go on out and pay Filthy a couple of months' rent and tell him I'll tack the damned linoleum down."

Chapter XVI

THERE was one hundred dollars' worth of bright-colored blankets on the big bed and the cot now, a radio that was as big as the fireplace in the living-room, two automatic shotguns and a rifle on the mantel and Keechie had a cigarette-case with a diamond in it. They had done a lot in four weeks. Old Filthy never did snoop around any more and just once had somebody come, Mrs. Philpott, the Salesman's wife, to borrow some sugar. Out here they never did see anybody except that little Philpott boy, Alvin, and then he was away down in the woods back of their place with a .22 rifle and that Spitz dog of his, Spots.

Bowie sat in front of the radio this evening, smoking the curved-stem pipe that Keechie liked, and thought how everything was looking pretty good. In that food-packed kitchen, Keechie was frying Irish potatoes the way he liked them, crisp and brown.

I don't care nothing about it myself, Bowie

thought, but we can start taking in some picture shows down there in that town pretty soon. Girls like to get out and go places. And that Law down there? I got him spotted and he ain't never going to get close to me.

In the darkened living-room, the flames of the fireplace logs splashed on the ceiling and walls. Had he brought in the wood tonight? Yes. What time was it? *Seven-thirty*. Christ, that Mexican orchestra Keechie liked was on. Bowie switched the dial. This was the station all right, but now they were talking about them damned constipation crystals.

If they were jumped now and had to rabbit, this radio and everything would have to be left behind. Well, I'm no damned soda skeet making ten dollars a week. I'll buy another one. Five hundred-dollar one and two hundred dollars' worth of blankets and if we go busted I know where I can get plenty more.

He placed another log on the fire and sat back down. The prongs of light shadow-boxed now on the walls, hooking and jabbing frenziedly. The orchestra was playing and Bowie got up and went back to the kitchen. Keechie was standing in front of the oven with a cloth in her hand.

"Hear that piece?"

Keechie nodded. *"La Golondrina."*

"Always makes me kind of sad somehow. Makes me think of them boys."

"Why?"

"I don't know. I been thinking about Chicamaw though, Keechie. I don't know whether I did that boy right or not up there in Keota, Keechie. He might have been expecting me to wait for him there and I didn't leave him no note or nothing."

"How were you going to leave him a note?"

"I don't know."

"Well, quit worrying about it then."

"I was just thinking about them."

"You have somebody else to worry about now."

"We just all started out together and you can't keep from thinking about things like that."

Bowie went back to the living-room and sat down. The fire had lowered and its glow filtered the darkness like a luminous screen. A cowboy singer was yodeling now about the prairie.

I do have to meet them boys in Gusherton, Bowie thought. They never did let me down and I sure can't go back on them. Why, they would just wait and wait and wait on me and I wouldn't let them do

189

that. She will understand. You will understand, won't you, honey?

The cowboy was singing *Nobody's Darling but Mine:*

> *Goodbye, Goodbye, Little Darling,*
>   *I'm leaving this Old World behind.*
> *Oh promise me that you will never*
>   *Be Nobody's Darling, but Mine. . . .*

Bowie cut the Voice off. I wish we could get more newspaper news over this and not that Mussolini and Africa and Congress and stuff like that. No news is good news though. If anything had happened to them boys, we would have heard about it.

Keechie called him. On the enameled table there were black-eyed peas, corn bread, fried potatoes, pineapple preserves and black coffee.

After supper, Bowie took the galvanized-iron tub of hot water off the stove and carried it into the living-room and lowered it to the floor in the hearth's glow. Keechie was going to take a bath.

He spread the bath mat and towels on the hearth around the tub and then looked around the room. The blinds were pulled close all right.

Standing, her naked thighs and legs glinted through the tub's rising vapors. She's sure filling out, Bowie thought. Now she raised her left arm and the soaped, dripping cloth in her right hand moved toward the shadowed pit. "I didn't know you were a such hairy little thing," he said.

Her arm came down. "Do you think I should shave?"

"I should say not. I like it. Don't you ever do it."

"I won't then. As long as I have you."

The whipping, drying towel covered and revealed and Bowie felt the heat of her burnished body glow in his eyes. He got up and picked up the white flannel pajamas off the radio. They smelled of clean soap. He handed them to her.

"Are you going to wash your feet tonight?" she said.

"Not tonight, honey. I washed them last night."

They lay under the warm, soft blankets now and Keechie's fingers played in the flannel over his chest. Outside, on the narrow cement walk, wind-kicked leaves scraped and scurried. In the daytime, he had watched the leaves leave the oak and they had twisted and spiraled to the ground like birds shot with an airgun.

She lay quietly now and he said softly: "Keechie?"

She half raised. "What is it, Bowie? Did you call me?"

"I thought you were asleep."

She peered at him hard. "What is it?"

"Nothing, honey. I didn't go to wake you up."

"What is it, Bowie?"

Distant, tiny, taut wires trilled in Bowie's ears. "I just been thinking."

"About what?"

"Just about things in general. Got to thinking about some of the boys up there in Alky. They come in there, Keechie, bragging about the women they got Outside waiting for them and after a little while they hush up and there's nothing more heard about it."

"I don't know anything about that."

"It doesn't make any difference, I don't suppose. I don't care what kind of a man you take. A doctor or a big college professor or any kind of a man and let him die and pretty soon his wife will be out running around with somebody else. These widows are just about as bad as any kind of a woman."

"I don't know about women like that."

"Some of these women bury a man and in no time at all pick right up with another. There's women,

Keechie, that will take up with a dozen men in their lives. Just one right in after another."

"Those women didn't love."

"Well, I don't know about that now, Keechie. They are bound to have been pretty crazy about them and maybe they didn't love all of them, but they loved some of them."

"A woman just loves once."

"What makes a woman live with one man a while and then with another one and then just run around with four or five more?"

"They just don't love."

"They must like it, Keechie, or they wouldn't do it."

"I don't know why other women do things. Maybe they are just looking and can't find anybody and then I guess some of them marry for a living."

"It just looks like to me that every woman will do it."

"I don't know what other women do."

"Now what would you do, Keechie, if I got in a little trouble somewhere and you and me might not be able to see each other again?"

Keechie did not say anything. The tiny wires

were as loud as crickets now and they swarmed in Bowie's ears. "Didn't you hear me?"

"There wouldn't be anything for me after you were gone. There is no use to think about that."

"Keechie, look at all these other women. Maybe they don't the first year and maybe they go two or three or four years, but pretty soon you see them lettin' some man slobber all over them."

Keechie was quiet.

"Now what do you have to say to that, Keechie?"

"I guess a woman is kind of like a dog, Bowie. You take a good dog now and if his master dies that dog won't take food from anybody and he'll bite anybody that tries to pet him and if he goes on, he'll rustle his own food and a lot of times he will just die too."

"You know that's right?"

"A bad dog will eat out of anybody's hands and take things from anybody."

"That's those big thoroughbred dogs that cost a pile of money that do that I guess. Them are real dogs."

"Maybe they do. I never did see, I don't guess, a real thoroughbred. The dog I am thinking about was there in Keota. I don't know what he was. No-

body else I don't guess. Old Man Humphrey owned
him and after he died I felt so sorry for that dog.
But he wouldn't have anything to do with anybody
and he wouldn't eat or drink and then he just died
too."

"I'll be doggone, Keechie. You know that's right.
It just goes to show you. You know, honey, you are
the smartest little old thing I ever did see."

"I'm not smart."

"You're a Little Soldier that's what you are."

"You go to sleep now."

The ringing in Bowie's ears faded far, far away
and his eyes grew heavy and he closed them. . . .

Chapter XVII

THE back yard of *Welcome Inn* had the width of an alley and then a fence of barbed wire and beyond that was ranch land, sage-grass and broomweed; far-reaching woods of green, pollen-blowing cedars and gray-trunked scrub-oaks. In it, long-horned, white-faced cattle grazed and sometimes one would come to their fence and nose in the rusty iron drum of burned cans and garbage. Once, Keechie had seen a doe and she called Bowie, but when he got to the back door, it was gone. Away to the south, beyond the woods, the Hills embossed the sky in a great, crawling circle. This evening, the sinking sun had flushed the horizon to a pretty pink like Keechie's underthings.

They sat now on the back steps of the cottage, Keechie in the coat of Bowie's gray suit. She was funny that way, always wearing something of his and even sleeping at nights in one of his shirts and he had paid fifteen dollars for that negligee and boudoir slippers.

Keechie pointed now and in the woods they saw the Philpott boy, Alvin, and the dog.

"I been kind of wanting to get out there with that kid some evening," Bowie said. "I never have seen him bringing back anything."

"He's having a good time though," Keechie said.

"Guess I just got too much else to think about." He tapped the bowl of his pipe on his palm and then slung the charred tobacco with a finger-spreading movement and wiped his hand across his thigh. The lining of his mouth felt thin and his tongue needle-pointed. I'll tell her after we go in, he thought. Only four days now and I got to be in Gusherton. That's all there is to it.

"Alvin yonder made me think of the little girl who used to live down on the corner from my Aunt. She died."

"Huh," Bowie said.

"She was awfully pretty. She used to say pieces in the church and her Mama fixed her up so pretty. It liked to have killed her Mama and I guess it was the reason that her Father went crazy. He was crazy before that, I would say though. He was a printer and he saved gold pieces. Every bit of money he saved he would go to the bank and get gold

198

pieces. Go up in the front room at nights and sit at a table and count it and look at it. His wife told him that it was going to bring bad luck."

"And then the kid died?"

"And it took every bit of the gold he had saved to pay for the funeral."

Bowie started filling his pipe. "Chicamaw was telling me about that lawyer friend of his he knew down in Mexico. Hawkins. That lawyer didn't believe in this heaven or hell stuff and said that the only way a man lived on was through his children. That was as far as this After-Life business went."

"Is that why you would like to have children?"

He looked at her. "Why, I never said nothing about having children."

"I know it."

"Why, would you like to have a baby?"

"Some day, maybe."

"Some day is right."

She stood up on the step and pulled the coat about her throat. "I'm satisfied now."

The match snapped and he flipped it and felt in his pocket for another. "No, a baby wouldn't have very much business with us."

"Well, if it couldn't be with us, I'd rather for it to be just you and me."

It was getting dark. The storm-broken limb yonder on the big oak-tree was twisted about the trunk like a petrified snake.

Bowie got up, knocking the unlighted tobacco out on the heel of his shoe. "I been thinking about the boys, Keechie. I guess I'll have to see them in a few days."

"Why?"

"A little business. I promised them I would meet them on the fifteenth of this month."

"Why?"

"Just business. I'll just be gone a couple of days and be back here before you know it."

"What are you planning on?"

"I just promised them, Keechie. That's all."

"What are you planning on doing?"

"Now I want you to understand, Keechie, that I'm not looking for trouble any more. I'm going up there, but I don't have anything in mind except just not let them boys wait and depend on me. We got a bank picked there all right, but I'm not planning on robbing it."

Keechie turned and grasped the door-knob. "I'm

going with you," she said. Then she went in the house.

He stood there alone. Up at the end of the row of cottages there was the sound of ax splitting wood. After a little while, he went in the house.

She lay on the bed in the darkness of the sleeping-room and he went over and sat on its edge. "No, you are not, Keechie," he said.

She did not say anything. She got up and went to the kitchen and he listened to the sound of water running in a glass. Presently, she came back.

"I said you weren't going," he said.

"I heard you."

"Well, quit running around when I'm talking to you."

She sat down on the bed beside him.

"Being in my heat is bad enough and you're certainly not going to get around three of us. I made up my mind about that a long time ago."

"All right, Bowie."

"Now let's get this straight. What do you mean all right?"

"I mean it will be all right."

"How are you going to be feeling when I come back?"

"All right."

"You are going to be here, aren't you?"

"Yes."

"And it is all right?"

Keechie got up and took his coat off, folded it and laid it on the bed rail. "You are keeping your promise and when you get up there you are going to let them know you are through with all that kind of business?"

"After Gusherton, I'm through."

"You know that I expect that, Bowie?"

"I sure do."

"All right then."

Keechie went into the kitchen and Bowie heard the wick of the oil stove sputter and then the rattle of the kettle on the flames. He lay down on the bed. After a little while the water in the kettle began to simmer. It sounded like a whimpering baby.

Chapter XVIII

THE front door of the Gusherton house parted and there was the smell of cold bacon and raw onion and then in the crack of light was Lula's water-color face. The door opened farther and Bowie went in and now he was shaking T-Dub's rocklike hand.

"Where's Chicamaw?" Bowie said.

T-Dub nodded toward the rear of the house. "Sleeping one off."

"For God's sake don't wake him up," Lula said. She had on a green velvet dinner gown that reached her ankles, and was adjusting a gold earring in her lobe. "I will absolutely leave."

"He sure has been guzzlin' it, Bowie," T-Dub said. "I don't know what's going to become of that boy."

"He's sleeping, is he?" Bowie said.

"Don't you wake him up now," Lula said.

Bowie lowered himself to the studio couch, balancing his hat on his close-pressed knees. T-Dub looked tired: like the morning they had walked the railroad ties all night. "Take his hat, Lula," he said. "Boy, you act like you just dropped in to say hello."

"I've been traveling pretty long and fast today," Bowie said. He watched Lula carry the hat and place it on the table by the door under the mirror.

"Where you been keeping yourself, Bowie?"

"Down south of here. Say, Chickamaw has been drinking a whole lot?"

"Oh, Christ, man. He brought an old bat in here last night that I'll swear to God he must have picked up in Nigger Town. Right in this house with Lula here."

"She was as drunk as he was and of all the goings-on," Lula said. "I told T. W. there that if you weren't here by nine o'clock tonight I was packing up and going to the hotel."

"She was too drunk to notice anything," T-Dub said. "That was one thing and as soon as he passed out I took her out and dumped her."

Lula had the other earring adjusted now and she smiled at Bowie. "We have something to show you and if you will just sit there I'll bring it right back."

"Okeh," Bowie said.

Lula disappeared in the back. "She has been

prettying up for two hours just because you were coming, I think," T-Dub said.

"How you been gettin' along, T-Dub?"

"Just gettin' by. Chicamaw had to go over day before yesterday to MacMasters and get fifty dollars off that lawyer friend of his to buy us gasoline and something to eat."

"You don't mean you have throwed all that, do you?"

"I got a family on my back, Bowie. I sunk twelve thousand dollars in a tourist camp over in MacMasters for that bud of mine and Mattie."

"How is he?"

"We've had hard luck about him. The parole board turned him down. I think that next year, though, he'll make it."

"That's too bad. I guess poor old Mattie is still up in the air."

"Me and Lula have been having a pretty good time too. In that New Orleans. Money will just naturally get away from you fast down there."

"Chicamaw been with you?"

T-Dub shook his head. "I thought he was with you all the time and then I figured too that he wasn't.

But I haven't seen him. He showed up here three nights ago it was. Drinking jake."

"I'll swear. I wish he would ease up on that drinking a little."

Lula came in. She had a roll of parchment-looking paper tied in a red ribbon and she looked at T-Dub now. "Do you want me to show it to him?"

T-Dub was grinning and his head went up and down.

Lula, smelling of fresh perfume, bent toward Bowie, unrolling the parchment and then spread it on his knees. It was a Marriage License.

"Did you two go and get hitched?"

T-Dub's head was still going up and down.

"Why, you got your right name on here, T-Dub," Bowie said.

"Just turned the initials around. W. T. Masefeld."

"That sure floors me," Bowie said. He handed the license back up to Lula.

"How are you and that little Oklahoma girl getting along?" T-Dub said.

Bowie's eyes quivered. "Who is that?"

"What's her name? Keechie. Keechie Mobley?"

"What do you know about her?"

"You remember, Bowie. I met her when we were all up there at Dee's place. I didn't know though that you two had teamed up until I begin to see that stuff in the papers."

Bowie's Adam's apple ached like it had been hit and he could not swallow. "What stuff is that?"

"Haven't you been seeing any of it?"

Bowie shook his head.

"I read something just last Sunday I think it was," Lula said. "Had her picture."

"Picture?" Bowie said.

"Why, hell, Bowie, I thought you knew all about that. That Dee Mobley up there claims you kidnaped her and I told Lula here that all that guy had done was yellowed up. Some Law got to pumping him and he just about let out that kind of a squawk. I told Lula here that that was the way it was. I knew damned well you wouldn't kidnap anybody. I mean a girl like that."

"And it's in the papers?" Bowie said.

"The last one was just last Sunday," Lula said. "It was a picture of her, I know, that she had taken when she was going to high school."

"Huh," Bowie said.

"It will die down, Bowie. I wouldn't let it worry me."

"It don't worry me."

Lula went over and sat crosswise on T-Dub's legs; he spread them and she lay against him and put her arm around his neck, the Marriage License roll in her left hand.

That means you and me have come to the parting of the ways, Little Soldier, Bowie thought. You can't be running with me no more.

T-Dub and Lula made a smacking sound as they kissed.

You can go on back up to Oklahoma and get everything squared up, Bowie thought. Let them think what they want. You have some money now, Little Soldier, and you can tell that old man of yours to go straight to Burning Hell.

"You go on back and pretty up some more, Sugar," T-Dub said. "Bowie and me want to talk a little business."

"Don't you go and get a headache now," Lula said.

I'd like to see some Law bother you while I'm gone, Bowie thought. Lay just one finger on you. I'll take care of myself, Brother Law, but you lay one finger on that girl and goddamn you, I'll get a machine gun and hunt *you* down!

Lula disappeared in the back of the house.

"This bank here is a bird's-nest on the ground," T-Dub said. "And it will go for fifty thousand or not a dime."

"I can use money," Bowie said. "A man never knows when he's going to need money and plenty of it in this business."

"You're not going to get three boys like us together every day," T-Dub said. "That is the way I look at it."

"And Chicamaw has been feeling pretty low?"

"Bowie, I think he would charge that bank tomorrow by himself if you and me both backed out."

"Well, he won't have to do it by himself."

.   .   .   .   .

They robbed the First National Bank of Gusherton at *10:01* o'clock the following morning, Chicamaw looking like a man with galloping consumption and driving Bowie's car; T-Dub complaining of rheumatism. There were no rumbles and at *10:15* they were switching cars, setting a match to Bowie's machine, and at *10:30* Chicamaw drove T-Dub's car,

T-Dub and Bowie crouched in the back, into the garage of their house at the edge of the city. Chicamaw went on in the house and fifteen minutes later T-Dub and then, after another interval, Bowie.

The bank went for only seventeen thousand dollars.

At noon, T-Dub fried bacon and eggs and made toast, but only Chicamaw ate. Bowie drank coffee.

That afternoon there was a football game on the radio and Bowie lost ten dollars to Chicamaw.

"You guys give me the jitters," Chicamaw said. "Why don't you say something?"

"You need a drink," T-Dub said.

"I need something to taper off on and just as soon as it gets dark I'm going to town and get it."

A little before dusk a car entered the driveway and they picked up guns, but it was only some damned bastard turning around to go back to town.

At dusk, T-Dub said he was going up to the first Drug Store and give Lula a ring at the Red Bonnet Hotel. "I might just go on down and pick her up and we'll shell out for New Orleans right tonight. You want to go down with me, either one of you?"

"I do," Chicamaw said.

"If you boys are going, I think I'll just go with

you too," Bowie said. "You can just drop me off at the bus station. I got some business to attend to and I want to get it over with."

Chicamaw had his hat on his head. "Why don't you hang around with us some, Bowie? I believe you're getting stuck up or something."

"I'll see you boys pretty soon."

"You want to watch yourself on these busses," T-Dub said.

"When I get down the line a couple of hundred miles I'll hop off and get me a car," Bowie said.

T-Dub named the night club on Bourbon Street in New Orleans and said he and Lula would be in it the night of December first.

"Okeh," Bowie said. "I guess you'll be there too, Chicamaw?"

"If I don't stump my toe," Chicamaw said.

The child in the shrunken coat slid off the Waiting Room bench, stood there, the drawers leg hanging, her hands behind her, looking at Bowie. He winked again. The child approached and when she got close, she thrust out her hand, palm up, fingers stretched.

"Oh, you want a nickel?" Bowie said.

The mother got up, a woman in a faded red coat with a cheap fur collar, and came toward them with her hands outstretched. "Is she bothering you?" she said.

"I should say not. Where are you going, Little Lady?"

"Grandpa's," Little Lady said. She extended the other hand now. "Why of all things, honey," the woman said.

Bowie placed the quarter on the child's palm and the fingers closed about it. "How about you sittin up here by me a little while?" Bowie said. He patted the bench. The child looked at the coin and then up at her mother. The woman helped her up on the bench.

The hard heels of the Policeman scraped on the tile floor toward the ticket window and he talked for a moment with the clerk there and then turned and moved back toward the door. At the door, he stepped back and then aside and two girls in fur coats, carrying week-end bags entered, a man in a tweed topcoat following. The Policeman went on out and the girls and the tweed-coated man stood at the ticket window now.

Bowie carried Little Lady in his arms, and inside

the crowded bus a bald-headed man in the third
seat got up and gave Bowie and the Mother his seat.

The woman talked. The skin in the hollows of
her eyes had the coloring of tobacco-stained cigarette
paper. She said her husband was a barber and
couldn't find work and she was going now to her
father until things got better. The child was just
getting over a bad cold.

Little Lady slept on Bowie's lap and now he
shifted her a little so her head would not touch the
hardness of the gun under his arm. The mother
said she was hoping her husband had work by
Christmas.

The finger-nails of Little Lady's limp fingers were
black-rimmed and looked like paper. Keechie's nails
were always clean and rounded short and pretty; not
long and sharp like Lula's. The night before he
left she had trimmed his toe-nails. All right now,
Big Boy, don't start that stuff. . . . Now this woman
here was having a tough time. She could stand a
little piece of money and here he was with almost
six thousand dollars on him.

The Mother was silent now, her head pressed
back against the seat, eyes closed. Pasteboard
showed through the paint of the purse on her lap.

What if he slipped a twenty in that purse? If he picked up that purse and she grabbed out and started yelling? It would win the fur-lined bathtub. It would bring him luck to get some money in that purse though. If he got five twenty-dollar bills in that purse and she didn't wake up it would break any jinx that was waiting up this road here. If he counted to thirteen and got five twenties in that purse there wouldn't anything stop him on this trip.

The woman was snoring now, the money in her purse.

A little after daybreak, Little Lady and her Mother left the bus and at eight o'clock, in San Angelo, Bowie got off and at ten o'clock he was driving south in the new automobile.

The clouds above the lowering sun looked like a picture of sea waves in the moonlight. A tiny flame was burning in Bowie's stomach. I've got to eat something. I haven't had anything to eat since. . . . Jesus Christ . . . I haven't eaten since day before yesterday. I'll be doggoned. I'm going to fool around and starve myself to death. Thinking about other things and here I am starving myself to death.

The sign read: *EATS*. Bowie drove into the broad parkway and stopped close to the screened door of the roadside lunch stand, a low, frame structure plastered with tin beer signs.

Bowie went in. There were a counter and five stools and a playing electric gramophone by a slot machine. A man in a white apron came from the back through the arched door and moved up inside the counter. The face of a woman peered through the kitchen slot.

"Soft boil me two and coffee," Bowie said. He straddled the first stool.

The man had a double chin, lumpy and soft-looking like the belly of a frog.

The gramophone was playing *El Rancho Grande*. Next to the cash register, held by the bottle of catsup and white mustard jar, was a folded newspaper. Bowie reached toward the newspaper and then brought his hand back. To hell with them damned newspapers.

The music ended and the machine made a clicking sound and was still. Frog Chin moved around the cash register and presently the coin slot jingled and then the machine was playing again: *El Rancho Grande*.

Bowie stirred the soft-boiled eggs and then broke

crackers and dropped the crumbs into the glass. He got the salt and pepper and then picked up the newspaper. It was a San Antonio paper. He took a bite and then spread the front page:

GUSHERTON, Texas, Nov. 16—One bandit was dead here tonight, another wounded and the wife-accomplice of the slain desperado was in jail as a vengeful aftermath of the bold, $17,000 holdup of the First National Bank here this morning.

The dead bandit is T. W. (Tommy Gun) Masefeld, escaped Oklahoma convict and sought for two months in connection with a half-dozen bank robberies in West Texas. He was shot to death by officers as he sat in a car parked in front of the Red Bonnet Hotel. His companion, Elmo (Three-Toed) Mobley, badly wounded, was in the hospital here under heavy guard.

Bowie A. Bowers, fast-triggered killer and leader of the bank bandit gang, had still eluded late tonight the combing search of a posse that numbered more than 300 peace officers and outraged citizens.

Mrs. Lula Masefeld, reputed wife of the slain bandit, was captured a few minutes after the shooting and lodged in jail.

The downtown gun battle terrorized scores of pedestrians and sent motorists scurrying for safety. The officers beat their quarry to the draw and neither bandit was able to fire.

Ten thousand dollars of the First National Bank loot was recovered in the bullet-riddled automobile. Credit for the heavy blow against the gang was being given tonight to Hotel Detective Chris Lawton. It was he who secured the tip that resulted in the laying of a trap for the bandit gang.

"What's the matter," Frog Chin said, "aren't them eggs all right?"

"Sure," Bowie said. He dipped the spoon into the glass.

At least three men and possibly two women participated in the sensational robbery here. Two bandits, identified as Bowie Bowers and Masefeld, entered the bank at 10 o'clock, forced a half-dozen bank workers and officials and a dozen customers into the vault at the points of six-shooters, rifled the safe and tills and escaped in the waiting car of confederates. Witnesses who saw the bandit machine speed away declared there was a woman in it.

Bowers, who escaped from the Oklahoma Penitentiary while serving a life term for murder, is wanted in connection with the murders of two Texaco City peace officers and a half-dozen bank robberies in Oklahoma, Kansas and Texas. Phantom-like, he has been seen traveling about the country in high-speed motor cars with a woman companion, said by Oklahoma authorities to be Keechie Mobley, cousin of the bandit wounded and captured here tonight.

"Those eggs done enough for you?"

"Fine," Bowie said. He took a bite and the food was like the man's phlegm in his mouth.

A woman is believed to have figured in Bowers' escape in Texaco City just as authorities here believe his disappearance here was abetted by a woman.

Mobley was suffering from wounds in the head and chest, but attending physicians declared he had a fighting chance to live. If he survives, however, he faces the electric chair. District Attorney Herbert Morton announced here tonight that he would ask the supreme penalty in the event Mobley went to trial.

"I loved Tommy more than anything in the world," pretty 19-year-old Lula Masefeld sobbed in her jail cell tonight. "He was the best thing in the world to . . ."

Bowie folded the newspaper and placed it back behind the bottle and jar. Then he got up and reached in his pocket before the cash register.

"It is getting so that you can't please anybody these days," Frog Chin said.

"I just wasn't hungry," Bowie said.

As he walked toward the car, his feet felt like clumps of prickly pear.

Chapter XIX

THE green-shaded lamp in the kitchen of *Welcome Inn* was burning, their signal that there had been no rumbles while he was gone, and now he closed the car door quietly and the leaves on the walk crackled under his moving shoes. He lifted on the knob so the door would not scrape and went in. Pale coals studded the mound of dark ashes in the fireplace and then he saw Keechie sitting on the end of the cot by the shadowy radio.

"I'm back," he said and he had the feeling that no sound had left his mouth and the words were melting in his hollow stomach. He strained: "I saw the light burning. You remembered all right."

"I did not know whether you were coming back or not," Keechie said.

He went over and stood on the hearth, clasping his hands behind him. Water dripped in the kitchen sink. "How has everything been?"

"All right."

The motor of a speeding car away over on the highway beat like a tom-tom.

"You want me to turn that light off in the kitchen?" Bowie said.

"If you want to."

"It doesn't matter. It really doesn't make any difference to me."

"I don't see that it makes any difference whether you came back here or not."

The heat at the base of his skull ignited and a film, like smoke, burned his eyes. "Oh, you mean about me, I guess?"

"Yes."

"Everything has happened pretty fast," he said. "Before you could say Jack Robinson, everything happened. You know about it?"

"Yes."

"About you?"

"Yes."

He moved toward her. "Doggone it, Keechie. I didn't mean for you to get mixed up in a business like this."

"Don't you worry about me."

He stopped.

"I will have to learn to take care of myself."

"All that old money is yours, Keechie. It will take care of you. Just don't go back around that . . . that old man of yours."

"I am not going back there. Don't worry about that."

"You will have to go back there, I guess. But don't you worry about that business. Them god-damned dingbats can't put nothing on you, nothing in this God's world."

"When did you start thinking about me?"

"Thinking about you?"

"You surely didn't think about me when you were gone?"

"Didn't think about you while I was gone?"

Keechie stood up. "You lied to me. *Lied.*"

"Why, Keechie." He moved toward her. "Why, you don't understand, Keechie."

"Don't you touch me." Her fists were clenched. "You took them. It was me or them and you knew it and you took them."

He lowered his hands. "I don't like to talk about them boys."

"They don't mean anything to me. They never did. You knew that. All right, you and me are through."

She was going toward the door now and he saw that she had on the cravenette coat and there was her two bags on the floor. "Where are you going?" he said.

"What does it matter to you?"

He reached her, bent and grasped the wrist of the hand reaching for the bag. She wrenched from him. "I told you not to touch me."

"You wait a minute," he said.

She stood there, making breathing sounds like her nostrils were stopped.

"You want to leave this way?" he said.

"Absolutely."

"Sore like this?"

"Whatever you want to call it."

His groin felt like it was emptying.

"Is that all?" Keechie said.

"You wait a minute."

"You won't stop me."

"No, I won't stop you, but you just wait a minute."

She stood there and now he turned and went over to the fireplace and looked at the smothering coals. He went into the kitchen and came back with crumpled papers and kindling and he scattered the ashes and placed them on the coals. The papers blazed and then he arranged sticks of wood on the flames.

"You don't have any business leaving this time of night," he said. "If anybody is going to leave this house, it's me."

"I'm not staying here."

"All right. Now I'm going to get it straight after a while. If you just have to go, all right. Now I'm going out this door here and I'm going to be gone on a long walk and if nothing will do you, but you have to go, there's a car out there and the keys are in it and you know where the money is."

"I don't want anything of yours."

"Don't be a damned fool." The knob grated with his wrench and he went out the door.

A bulbous crescent hung heavily in the bottom of the moon's slate-colored disk. Wind gushed in the trees with the sound of a distant river and the tops of the cedars, silhouetted against the cobalt and starlit heavens, whipped and threshed like tiny Christmas trees in a storm. He walked now on the gray wood-cutters' road that twisted and slashed deep into the woods.

This is what you wanted, isn't it, Big Boy? It had to stop some time and what's the difference how it happened? You just keep going down this road and walk, by God, until these damned legs of yours come off. *Keechie in front of the oil heater in the Bunk, floor dust tatting the hem of her skirt.* All right now, don't start that stuff.

The wind's chill crawled under his trouser cuffs and down the neck of his collar and he turned up his lapels. I have plenty of things to do. Nothing in this old world will do you any more good, T-Dub, but, Chicamaw, you got a friend. Don't you think different for a minute, boy. You're just as liable as not to be running these roads again with me pretty soon and it's not going to be any year from now.

His shadow glided on the road beside him, stubby and slender. *Keechie picking cigarette butts off the floor to make him a smoke with a cigarette paper she had found.* Now lay off that stuff, goddamit. What difference does it make how it happened, just so it happened? Okeh. Okeh. Okeh. *Okeh!*

The broken tree stump yonder with its two short, outflung limbs looked like a man. Bowie pressed his hand against the gun's butt in the holster under his arm. Hell, I don't need a gun with one Law. Brave men. Heroes. Fifty of them to get one Thief,

224

hundred, two hundred, three hundred. Big Shots. Heroes.

A plummeting meteor fragment streaked the heavens like the spark of a shaken log, vanished. That means you're gone, Little Soldier. That means you have left.

He left the woods now, moved across the clearing toward *Welcome Inn,* in a dawning mist that blew like sifted ashes. The car stood where he had left it. Christ, girl, you didn't leave this place walking? Now you didn't do *that.* Why, girl, you're liable to get in trouble. . . . Smoke was coming from the chimney.

She sat in front of the burning logs, smoking a cigarette, her coat off. "I couldn't leave," she said.

His neck was rigid, fixed; he could not move it.

"I couldn't leave," she repeated.

"I noticed the car out there," he said.

"There wasn't anything for me Out There," she said. "Nothing. *Nothing!*"

Bowie placed his hand on her shoulder, patted. "You ought to turn in."

"I guess so."

"That is what I would do."

After a little while, Keechie got up and moved

toward the sleeping-room and he followed; stood in the doorway and watched her lie down on the bed. Then he went over and sat on the edge.

"I didn't want to leave you," Keechie said.

His head went up and down.

"You wouldn't have let me go, would you, Bowie?"

"No."

"Even if I had wanted to?"

"No."

"You would have made me stay?"

"Yes."

"I help you, don't I, Bowie?"

"Yes."

"A whole, whole lot?"

"Yes."

Keechie closed her eyes and presently she sucked in a deep breath through her mouth and nose, jerked convulsively and he placed his hands on her. She jerked again, easier though, and now her mouth was closed and she slept. Bowie took the gun out of his holster and placed it just under the edge of the bed, loosened his tie, unbuttoned his collar. Then he lay down beside her.

Chapter XX

KEECHIE said it looked like Santa Claus would have to come this year in a boat instead of a sleigh. It had rained for six days. In the daytime, the rain-shrouded woods and hills were merged with the sky and their cottage stood on a tiny island. They went to bed at night with the rain caressing their roof and awoke in the morning with it still beating a gentle, broken rhythm.

It was getting close to five o'clock this afternoon and any time now Alvin Philpott, the little boy, would be showing up with the San Antonio newspaper. Bowie had made a deal with him four weeks before, fifty cents a week, and every afternoon now, as Alvin came home from school, he brought a paper. They were going to get the boy something for Christmas. That was only four days off now.

"How would you like to have a little egg nogg for Christmas?" Keechie said. She stood there in the kitchen doorway, a sweet potato in one hand, a peeling knife in the other.

Bowie placed Keechie's polished oxford on the floor and picked up the other one. "Did you ever drink any of that?"

Keechie shook her head. "Maybe I did when I was little, I don't know. I just saw a recipe in the paper and I think nearly everybody drinks it around Christmas time. The eggs in it are good for you."

"If it's just the same to you," Bowie said, "we'll just get a quart of whisky and drink it straight. But no egg noggs for me. I got sick as a horse on it once and I swore to God in heaven that if I ever got over it, I would never drink no more egg nogg no more."

Keechie laughed and went back into the kitchen. They were going to have pork chops and candied sweet potatoes with marshmallows for supper.

Bowie rubbed the brown polish into Keechie's shoe. We'll do something Christmas all right, he thought. It won't be just like any other day. He had that Christmas present to his Mama off his mind now. One thousand dollars. He and Keechie had driven yesterday to San Antonio and mailed the envelope. There was one thing, though, he had to do pretty soon and that was get some money to that lawyer friend of Chicamaw's in MacMasters. Archibald J. Hawkins. He and Keechie would have to go back to San Antonio and attend to that. Two thousand dollars in an envelope to a lawyer? The guy might be dead and somebody else would get it? The thing to do was go in some bank in San Antonio and get a draft and send it to Hawkins. Lawyers knew better than to go south with a thief's money. That one in Tulsa had found that out. Now he could send Chicamaw a postal order for one hundred dollars. In the Christmas rush in them banks and post-offices in San Antonio, nobody would big-eye Keechie or him.

The screen rattled and Bowie got up and went to the door. It was Alvin. Water dripped from the boy's nose and he pulled the dry newspaper from underneath his soggy coat.

"You going to get wet, boy, if you ain't careful," Bowie said.

"It don't bother me," Alvin said.

After Alvin left, Bowie went back to the kitchen. "I know now what we will get that kid," he said. "A raincoat."

"That will be better than a shotgun," Keechie said.

There was nothing in the newspapers. There was enough in there day before yesterday, Bowie thought. Chicamaw was going to trial February fourth. That lawyer Hawkins sure had to have some money pretty soon because they would sure put the Chair on Chicamaw if he didn't get some money.

After supper, Keechie and Bowie played checkers. It was raining harder now, wind whistling in the window-screens and water splashing in the puddles under the eaves.

Bowie stacked the checkers in the box with the sliding top. "You know I been thinking, Keechie, about what you said the other day about it being easier for a woman to disguise than a man. I believe it's easier for a man when you get to thinking about it. A man can grow a beard and wear glasses and get his hair cut different."

"He can't use powder and paint though."

"He sure can. He can dress up like a woman and get by with it."

"I'd like to see you dressed up like a woman."

"Not me."

"And I'm not going to dress up like a man."

"I know it," Bowie said. "But you know, Keechie, there's men in this world though that go around all the time dressed up like women. They're no good."

"There was a woman in Keota that smoked cigars and acted just like a man," Keechie said.

"Them people are no good, Keechie. Absolutely. They're no good."

"There are more no-good people in this world than there are good ones," Keechie said. "A blind man can see that."

"Up there in Alky, Keechie, you never saw the like. You would never have thought so many no-good people could be gotten up all together at one time. That was one of the reasons why I just couldn't stand it there any longer. I don't know though, but what it's just about the same Out Here."

The window-screens whined and Bowie listened. Then he put his finger in his ear and jiggled it. "Yessir, Keechie, I think you hit the nail on the head when you said that the only way to beat this game was just go off and pull the Hole in after you. Not have a single friend."

"You can't trust anybody, Bowie."

"I've always said that, honey. I wouldn't trust Jesus Christ if he come right in this door right this minute."

"You just have to depend on yourself in this world and nobody else," Keechie said.

231

Bowie got up and placed the box of checkers and the board on the mantel. He turned, placed his elbows on the mantel's edge and pushed his stomach out away from the heat. "But you know, Keechie, you never will see three boys like us together again. I think about that Chicamaw up there in that jail pulling through by himself and I'll bet he doesn't even have cigarette money."

"Nobody but a lawyer can help him now."

"I know it. That's what I have been thinking about. I'll bet that boy is beginning to think that he doesn't have a friend in this world."

"There is nothing you can do about it. Unless you want to get him some money."

"That will do it, Keechie. It will do it nine times out of ten in this world. That's what I have to do. Get him a lawyer lined up. And a good one."

"You don't have to go anywhere around him though?"

"What are you talking about? I should say not. No, all I have to do is to get some mazuma to a good lawyer and that will be all there is to it."

Keechie got up and went over to the wood box. She carried the stick to the fireplace and said: "Move over a little, Bowie."

Sparks popped under the dropped wood and Keechie stood there watching the flames lengthen. "Don't that rain sound good, Bowie?"

"What did you say, Keechie?"

"I said don't you like to hear that rain on the house?"

"Uh huh. I sure do. You bet I do."

"I like it," Keechie said.

The floor planks creaked as Bowie began moving about. "I should have brought in more wood today," he said. "I guess this rain is just going to keep on forever."

.　　.　　.　　.　　.

On Christmas Eve morning, icicles hung from the eaves, but the day was breaking clear. The sun was going to shine. Bowie and Keechie lay in bed, talking now about how Alvin was going to act when they gave him the raincoat this afternoon. They had bought the raincoat in Antelope Center yesterday and also a half-dozen handkerchiefs that they were going to give Alvin to give to Filthy MacNasty.

"If we're going to go to San Antonio this morning and get back here by four o'clock, we got to be gettin' up and going," Bowie said. "We're not going to get any business done much less seeing a show at this rate."

"Well, I don't see nothing holding you down in this bed, Booie-Wooie," Keechie said.

"You usually get up before I do, don't you? What's got hold of your legs this morning? Can't you take them icicles this morning?"

"Sure. I was just waiting to see you show what a he-man you are. Why don't you get up and start the fire this morning?"

"Who, me?"

"I hope it's you and not somebody else I'm talking to."

"By God, I hope so too. Now let me see. All I got to do is just get up and sort of walk in there to that fireplace. All right, you win, Keechie-Weechie." Bowie swept back the covers, got out, tucked the blankets back under Keechie and trotted, barefooted, into the cold living-room.

In the kitchen, Bowie saw the flooded floor and then the burst pipe of the shower in the bathroom.

"I will go and get Filthy and tell him to phone a plumber," Keechie said.

"No, you just stay here," Bowie said. "I'll go."

It was ten o'clock when the rattling, banging Ford

pick-up with the vise stopped in front of the cottage. Bowie, the mop in his hand, stood at the window and watched the plumber get out. The man had a head shaped like an Irish potato and an unlit cigar stub in the corner of his mouth.

"You the folks that are having a little trouble out here?" Plumber said.

Bowie thumbed toward the back. "Bathroom."

Plumber looked at Keechie standing by the bed.

"In the bathroom," Bowie said.

Plumber's smile was soggy. The cigar stub darkened against his draining face. "We been swamped," he said. "Freeze. Bathroom?"

Bowie pointed.

Plumber moved across the living-room and into the hallway toward the bath.

Bowie turned and looked at Keechie.

Keechie framed the question with soundless lips: What do you think?

Bowie's head went up and down.

Plumber came out of the hallway walking briskly toward the door. "Tools," he said.

They watched him through the window. He got in the pick-up, started the motor and then the machine moved off with a violent jerk.

235

Bowie pointed at Keechie's coat. "Get on out and start our car."

Mud-thickened water geysered from the puddles at the Gate and splattered on their windshield. Bowie pressed the wiper button and then turned onto the highway. The road extended ahead, gray and slick as phlegm; gravel rattled under the fenders.

"Light me a cigarette," Bowie said.

Keechie looked in the panel pocket. "We don't have a one, Bowie, not a one."

"Can you beat that?"

"We will get some."

"Can you beat that. Now that's what I call luck for you. You mean to say there's not a one there?"

"We will get some, Bowie."

"Now that's what I call luck."

Thunder rolled. It was like the hills around them had been undermined and were bumping around.

"I'm sure fed up on rain," Bowie said. "I'm sure fed up on it."

"Where are we going, Bowie?"

"MacMasters."

"MacMasters?"

"I'm going to see a lawyer there."

"MacMasters," Keechie repeated.

The highway stretched on like a long ribbon of wet funeral cloth; the rain-drunk weeds of the right-of-way rushing behind.

"Alvin won't get his raincoat," Keechie said. "It was laying there on the radio."

Bowie cleared his throat. "I been thinking. It's a good thing we gassed up yesterday and got them cans filled. What if we were just starting out with a couple of gallons like we had yesterday morning? By golly, we sure got some gas in this buggy."

"We're lucky," Keechie said.

Chapter XXI

THE house of J. Archibald Hawkins, the lawyer, was a straight, two-story house with a porch of warped planks and next to the First Christian Church. In the furniture-stuffed Front Room, there was a roll-desk, its top stacked with law books of tan and red cloth; a piano with two hymn-books on the rack and framed portraits on the shawl-scarfed top. The worn places in the carpet looked like burlap sacking and on the square of cracked linoleum by the broad, sliding door a gas-stove ejected long, curling flames.

When Hawkins smiled, his eyes became wrinkled pockets and his cheeks looked like balls wrapped in cellophane. His Sister, who lived with him, had gone to Amarillo to see her son and it had looked like he was going to spend Christmas night alone. "It appears though," he said, "that I have some pretty distinguished company."

Bowie, sitting there on the claw-carved, leather divan grinned, and Keechie looked down and covered the strip of house dress over her legs with the coat's skirt.

"Now about Chicamaw again, Judge?" Bowie said.

"We will get him fixed up," Hawkins said. He did not practice criminal law himself, he added, but he knew personally the members of the Law Firm in Gusherton who could do something with the case. It would take money though.

"How much?" Bowie said.

Hawkins smiled. "Just about all they decide a man has."

"Around how much?"

"I know this firm will not take a case for less than two thousand."

"Say three thousand?" Bowie said.

Hawkins nodded. "It is a pretty good newspaper case too."

"I'd like to see Chicamaw get some money too. Think you can manage it?"

"I can see him very easily."

"And I'll leave you five hundred for all this trouble."

"I can certainly use it."

Bowie crossed his leg and leaned forward with his elbow on his knee and chin in hand. "You know anything how that happened in Gusherton? Them boys gettin' in trouble, I mean?"

Hawkins nodded. "Yes, I know. That girl. What is her name? Masefeld's wife."

"Good lord," Bowie said. "Sure enough?"

"It was pure simple-mindedness. That hotel detective over there made some advances that were unwelcome to her and, instead of ignoring them, she made a scene. Complained to the Manager and said she had a husband and plenty of money. It seems this hotel detective got suspicious then sure enough and plugged in on her telephone. He got the tip that way."

"I'll swear," Bowie said.

"She is going to testify for the State in Chicamaw's trial."

"I'll swear."

Keechie said they had better be going.

Hawkins said that he had a big chicken back there in the oven and it would only take a half-hour for it to warm. Wouldn't they keep an old man company a little on Christmas night?

Bowie looked at Keechie. She consented.

The lawyer talked. There are more millionaires in this country than in any other, he said, and at the same time more robbers and killers. Therein lay significance. Extremes in riches make extremes in crime. As long as a Social System permitted the acquisition of extreme riches, there would be equalizing crime and the Government and all law-enforcement organizations might as well fold their hands and accept it.

"The Rich," Hawkins said, "can't drive their big automobiles and flaunt bediamonded wives and expect every man just to simply look on admiringly. The sheep will do it and the sheep will even laud it and support it, but at the same time these sheep will feel something that they do not understand and demonstrate it and that is known as so-called glorification of the big criminal."

"I'm not proud of nothing I ever done," Bowie said.

Money interests fix the punishment for crime in this country, Hawkins said, and consequently there is no moral justice. A bum steals a pair of shoes from another and that is a great crime, but what will happen to the complaining bum at the police station? If that same thief pilfers fifteen cents from the telephone box of a big utility company, he can receive fifteen years, but if he snatches that amount from the cup of a blind beggar, he may get a twenty-dollar fine. . . .

Hawkins' stomach gurgled and Bowie looked down, saw the dried mud on the toe of his shoe and then looked at Keechie's shoes. There was mud on them too.

"Now you take the Stupid Sheep I was talking about a moment ago," Hawkins said, "just like this young fellow that lives right down here in a little two-room apartment across the corner from me. He drives a milk truck for a millionaire creamery man here and he works ten and twelve hours a day and he goes home at night and there is a baby that he has to help his wife with. His wife is sick. Still weak and unable to work from bearing that child. Now you take that boy. Is it strange that he doesn't feel what these newspapers yap about glorification of the criminal?"

"These newspapers never get nothing straight," Bowie said. "They got me working in towns that I have never even been inside of."

"There is nothing like a man hunt and trust the newspapers to make an arena and ballyhoo the Kill. The Romans were not cruel. At least no more cruel than these newspapers that get their readers' tongues

hanging out for the Kill. And just here last week
the Chamber of Commerce gave the Creamery Millionaire a silver loving-trophy as being MacMasters'
most useful citizen of the year. And the irony of it
all is that you take that fourteen-dollar-a-week boy
that is working for him and put him on a jury and
some Prosecutor who wants his name in the newspapers more than anything else will have that boy
thinking that red-hot spikes are too mild for a bank
robber."

"I get a kick out of robbing banks," Bowie said.
"I don't mind admittin' it."

Keechie touched the back of Bowie's hand. "It's
getting pretty late."

"We'll go in a minute, honey."

"We have some chicken coming up," Hawkins
said. "I bet you young folks think I am a long-
winded old cuss."

"Go on," Bowie said. "I like to hear you."

"Speaking of crime," Hawkins said. His stomach
gurgled. "There was a Consumptive that come
down here from Detroit in an old rattletrap here a
couple of months ago and he had two little dogs.
That is all that man had and he moved in a little
shack on the river down here close to town and then

that ranchman, who lived across the river and is worth, I guess, fifty thousand dollars, killed those two dogs with a shotgun and there is not a law in this state that will punish that cold-blooded, low-down, degenerate murderer."

" 'Fraid he would get a cow bit, I guess?" Bowie said.

"That. But that man shoots dogs down like he would rattlesnakes."

"They caught a fellow in the town I used to live in," Keechie said, "throwing weenies with poison in them out to dogs. He was just driving around town doing it."

Bowie looked at her. "You never did tell me about that," he said.

"Prisons are simply pimples on a corrupt world," Hawkins said. "The great criminals, I mean the real enemies of man's welfare and peace and happiness, never go near a prison and the dead ones, out in these cemeteries, have the highest tombstones over their heads. Normal men with abnormal tendencies. Abnormal men with normal tendencies. My God. It is a wonder people do not smell, their minds are so rotten. Excuse me, young lady."

"Them capitalist fellows are thieves like us," Bowie said. "They rob widows and orphans."

"I do not fool myself one minute," Hawkins said. "I possess that. You take me, Bowers, and that five hundred you have given me. I am going to run for Justice of the Peace this spring. When an old broken-down lawyer gets old, Son, he runs for Justice of the Peace."

"You don't look old," Bowie said.

"Anyway I am going into this next election and I rather think I am going to have that Office. I will get a couple of constables, gun-toters, and these boys will go out and break up Negro dice games, raid petty little home-brew joints in Mexican town and take in some of these tourists that are exceeding the speed limit by a few miles. We will make good fees. Vultures are all we are."

"I guess a man has to make a living," Bowie said.

"In this system he is forced to be a criminal."

"I never robbed nobody that couldn't stand to lose it," Bowie said.

Hawkins looked at Keechie. "And whatever road a man takes there is always a woman that will follow him."

246

"If this man here will just get up and start," Keechie said, "I will follow him right now."

"Don't pay no attention to her, Judge," Bowie said.

The gurgling sounded in Hawkins' stomach again.

The strung, colored lights of this town's Main Street illuminated an empty, quiet thoroughfare. On the Court House lawn, a big, lighted Christmas tree glowed greens and reds and yellows. The sign at the edge of the town read: *New Orleans . . . 590 mi.*

"You think we will be there this time tomorrow night?" Keechie said.

"Uh huh. Keechie, I can just see that Indian's face when them big lawyers start coming in his cell. He's sure going to know he's got a friend Out Here."

"You have done everything you could now."

Bowie turned his head toward her and grinned. "Say, did you hear Old Windy's guts growling?"

"I thought he was never going to stop talking."

"I never heard anything like it," Bowie said. "You could have heard it out in the street."

Chapter XXII

Bowie and Keechie had the renting of a furnished house on their minds when they entered New Orleans, but it was late and they were so tired that they looked at an apartment and there were so many nice things about the very first one that they took it. The place—*The Colonial Apartments*—was a remodeled home and as big as an old West Texas court house. On an avenue of palm-fenced homes and big churches, this house was shadowed and darkened by spreading cottonwoods and hackberries, and crêpe myrtles screened the windows.

Mrs. Lufkin was the owner of *The Colonial Apartments*. She was a stout-bosomed woman with dyed black hair and smelled like a brewery. Mrs. Lufkin did not have much to do with the running of the apartments, leaving this to Rebecca, the little Negro woman with gold teeth. From Rebecca, Bowie and Keechie learned about the other occupants of the place: the Professor who taught in the University up the avenue; the Interne and his Nurse-

Wife who were at the hospital most of the time; the four girls who lived in the two apartments upstairs and were students in the University. Rebecca said Mrs. Lufkin bought whisky five gallons at a time and she prayed for her every night.

The ceiling of their living-room was so high that Keechie could not touch the plastered dome even when Bowie lifted her. There was a wide, high fireplace of polished granite and a log gas-heater. In a few days, when they made that one big shopping tour downtown, they would get a radio to put beside the library table and beaded parlor lamp. And a red-checkered cloth for the kitchen table, Keechie said.

The sleeping-room had a tiled floor and in it were wedged a bed and a clear-mirrored vanity. The kitchen was small too, but it would look a lot better, Bowie said, when that big pantry was filled with stuff to eat. The bathroom was as big as the kitchen and steaming water gushed from the *hot* tap. Now you can get all the baths you want, Bowie said, and when Keechie said she had been thinking about that, Bowie said he did not see how they had put up with it back in those Texas hills.

They would get a telephone put in, they decided,

and any time there was drug-store buying or anything like that to do, they would have delivery boys bring it to their door. Rebecca had said that she went to the Grocery every morning and would be glad to get their things too. They would give her a few dollars a week, Bowie said, and that old black gal would break her neck for them. There would not be anybody to see except Rebecca and delivery boys and at nights they could duck in suburban picture shows.

The best thing about it all, Keechie said, was that no one in the world knew where they were. She lettered the slip that Bowie inserted in the slot of the mailbox in the lobby: *Mr. & Mrs. F. T. Haviland.*

When the trial of Chicamaw started back in Gusherton, Bowie waited in the kitchen every afternoon listening for the thump of the thrown newspaper on the back steps. There were three days of the trial and then on the fourth day, Bowie read in the Sunday-morning paper of its outcome. Chicamaw had beaten the Chair. He had drawn a pair of nines —ninety-nine years.

Bowie carried the newspaper back to Keechie who was still in bed this Sunday morning. "That boy beat them," Bowie said. "They're not going to kick any Switch off on him. It's right here in the paper, Keechie."

"I'm glad," Keechie said.

"Go ahead and read it, Keechie. Here it is, right here."

"Now you will feel a lot better," Keechie said.

"And don't think he is just sittin' up there in that jail with his brains sittin' too. And he won't have to kill anybody to beat that Pen either. Any day you want to kill somebody, Keechie, you can beat a Pen easy."

"That is none of your worry now."

"Go ahead and read it. I'll stir us up some breakfast. How about me cooking it up this morning? How about it?"

"All right."

By ten o'clock, sunlight was knifing through the crêpe myrtle and the raised windows, cutting bright squares on the living-room carpet and blue linoleum of the kitchen. This is one day I'm not going to stay cooped up, Bowie thought. We're going to get out. Keechie sat on the vanity bench with a curling iron in her hand. She had on the Chinese wrapper with the yellow and red dragon designs.

"Let's get out of this place today, Keechie. What do you say?"

"Where?"

"Don't make one bit of difference to me. Just so we go."

"Would you like to go walking in that Park up the avenue?"

"You're doggone whistling."

Keechie put the curling iron on the vanity and stood up. "I've always wanted to go through it in the daytime. I'll wear my gray flannel suit."

"I'll strut out in that double-breasted. Say, Little Soldier, you're getting as broad as I don't know what."

Keechie looked down her body, at her hips.

"You're puttin' on plenty," Bowie said.

"Don't you like it?"

"I should say I do. You could get as big as the side of a barn and I'd like it."

"Well, there's no danger of that."

The lower limbs of the big oak in the Park grew on the ground as if the task of going up was too much. The gray Spanish moss that fringed the boughs, Keechie said, was whiskers and showed how old the trees were. They circled the tree now and moved across the smooth fairway of the golf course, pausing near the fluttering pennant on the green, and then went on toward the lagoon. A couple passed ahead of them, a wire-haired terrier straining on a leash held by the woman. The man bent down now to tie a shoe-lace and then trotted to catch up.

"If I had a dog I would want one of them big police babies," Bowie said. "They're mean as hell."

Swans glided on the lagoon, the traced water smoothing behind them. Around the bend of water-dipping willows, a rowboat came, the oars splashing; three girls in it. The swans moved closer to the shore. On the boat were the letters *Nellie*. The girl rowing had on brown slacks and a white sweater. Bowie and Keechie lowered themselves to the grass of the bank's edge and watched the girls and the boat disappear around the bend below.

"What are you thinking about?" Keechie said.

"I had an aunt named Nell," Bowie said. "I was thinking about her."

"Your Daddy's sister?"

Bowie shook his head. "Mama's. We lived with her a while, I mean Grandma's, after my Dad got killed. It's funny that I got to thinking about her."

"What about her?"

"Oh, I don't know. She used to come on Sunday afternoons and bring a big old sack of red-hots and licorice drops and candy like that. You remember that kind of candy, don't you?"

Keechie nodded. She reached out and plucked a bit of grass from the silk of Bowie's socks.

"Makes me think of that boy I was running around with too then," Bowie said. "You know that kid, the last time I heard of him, was a big football player in Oklahoma University and he was just a cutter and a half. We were a pair now. His Dad was the County Treasurer in that town and why he was running around up back alleys and gettin' junk and sellin' it, I don't know. That boy had more devilment in him than anybody I ever did know. We got to going in vacant houses and tearing the plumbing out and selling the brass and lead. I remember one day we made eighty cents. We bought four of them nickel pies apiece. That kid always had money in his pockets. He would steal it out of his Dad's pants at nights."

Keechie plucked a blade of Bermuda grass and began chewing the white root.

"I don't know how come me to ever think of him,

but he just knew about everything that was going on in that town. That's how come me to go out to them houses at the edge of town one day. The Red Light district. He said there was women out there who would give kids nickels and dimes if they just went out there and hung around the back door."

The hoofs of running horses sounded and then on the bridle path, on the other side of the lagoon and through the trees, they saw the bright jackets of the women riders.

"I saw her, but I don't think that she knows to this day that it was me. When the old woman in the House started hollering at us to get away, she come to the back door and I saw her."

"Saw who?" Keechie said.

Bowie looked at her. "My Aunt. I thought I told you."

"Oh," Keechie said.

"She didn't recognize me though."

Keechie leaned against Bowie's leg, picked another bit of dead grass and smoothed the silk.

The horsewomen were passing yonder again, posting.

"Ain't that a helluva way to ride?" Bowie said. "Bobbing your bottom up and down like that?"

"Uh huh."

Bowie indicated the golf green behind them with a twist of his head. "That's something else I never figured why anybody could get interested in. Batting that little old ball around and puttin' it in holes."

"Some people don't have anything else to do," Keechie said. "It wouldn't bother me though if they stood on their heads if they were having a good time."

"Me neither."

They walked now along the lagoon's bank toward the white dome of the Memorial Band-stand. Bowie stopped and pointed at the rat swimming in the water toward the little island of weeping willows. "I'll bet that rat has him a Hole over there," he said.

"I didn't know rats could swim," Keechie said.

"Them kind can. I know one kind that can't do anything but snitch. Them are yellow and have two legs."

"Oh," Keechie said. "Now I get you."

"I can tell you something else about some of these boys that are gettin' in trouble every day," Bowie said. "They like to see their names in the newspapers. Why, Keechie, there's guys that will put on acts and do anything just to get their names big in the newspapers."

"I had just as soon talk about something else," Keechie said.

"Just one more thing, Keechie. Have you been thinking about us not gettin' our names in the paper no more? There hasn't been hardly one thing since that damned plumber flushed us back yonder in them damned old rainy hills."

"Just don't do anything to get your name in the paper," Keechie said. "That is the thing."

"Say we got jumped here, Keechie. Now I know. There isn't a chance just as long as we keep our noses clean like we're doing. But just say we were. Where would you like to go?"

"I don't know."

"You know where I would like to go? Mexico. It takes somebody, though, that knows the ropes to get you across that border and situated good down there. Now you take Chicamaw, he knew the ropes down there from A to Z."

"Well, Chicamaw isn't here and he isn't going to be here."

"I know it. I was just telling you, honey."

The couple coming across the narrow rustic

bridge were holding hands, and Bowie and Keechie stepped aside and gave them passageway. The girl had on a white silk dress and the black hair of the fellow grew long and curling down his neck. As they stepped off the bridge, the fellow put his arm around the girl supportingly.

Bowie and Keechie went on. "You can tell by looking at them they're not married," Bowie said.

"How can you tell?"

"I don't know. Just the way he was holding her hand as if she was going to fall off that bridge or something, I guess."

"Clever, aren't you?"

"I notice little things like that."

"Maybe she would have fallen off if he hadn't been helping her. Married or not married. A girl likes that anyway."

Bowie looked at her. "Say, do you want me to hold your hand like that?" He reached toward her. Keechie swept his hand down. "Just keep that to yourself," she said.

"Gollee, honey. What's come over you? What did I do?"

Keechie turned around. "Let's go home."

"Gollee, can you beat that. What have I done?"

Keechie started back and he caught up and walked alongside her again. Near the broad stone arch of the Park's exit, a bunch of boys, their shirt tails flapping, were playing with an indoor ball. Bowie asked Keechie to wait a minute and they stood there and watched the players a little while.

The sunshine was gone now and the air touched their bodies like cold feathers. The avenue would be quiet and then, with the spreading green of the green signal light down the thoroughfare, the gears of the waiting automobiles would grate and crash, and then they came, passing in rushing trains.

"I've been thinking about old T-Dub," Bowie said. "I guess that girl was just dumb. But you know they were like a couple of kids showing me that Marriage License."

"First I had heard about it," Keechie said.

"Didn't I ever tell you about that? Well, they were just like a couple of kids, dragging that License out and showing it all around."

"I guess it mattered to them."

Bowie looked at Keechie, a loosened curl moved on her upturned coat collar. "I guess it did," he said. "They were like a couple of kids."

A street-car crashed past, its trolley popping, a

glued mass of humanity through its closed windows.
At the intersection, Bowie touched Keechie's arm as
they stepped down off the curb."

"Would you marry me, Keechie?"

She looked up at him, then ahead again. "I don't
know whether I would or not."

"Now just what do you mean by that?"

"I can't see what difference some writing on a
scrap of paper makes if that's what you are thinking
about."

"I don't either. That's what I have been thinking. What difference does a piece of red ribbon
around some paper make? Besides, you're married
to me already if you didn't know it."

Keechie looked up at him again. "Where do you
get that?"

"It's the law, Keechie. Honest. If you intro-
duce a woman three times in public as your wife,
you're just as much married as if you had a Justice
of the Peace and nine preachers to do it. Honest.
That's the law and you can't get around it."

"I didn't know that."

"You take you and me now. All right, didn't
Filthy MacNasty get it that way and Mrs. Lufkin

up here and Rebecca and anybody that looks at that mail box? You can't get around it."

"I didn't know that."

"You can't get around it," Bowie said. "That's the law."

At the next crossing, he took her arm and held it the rest of the way home.

Chapter XXIII

FOR several days now Keechie had not been feeling well and this morning, after she smoked a cigarette, she felt sick at her stomach and had to lie down. Bowie rinsed towels under the cold tap in the kitchen and put them on her forehead.

It was only May, but the damp heat was like a jail cell in July. It clogged the nostrils and sweat streaked Bowie's cheeks from his sideburns. He said it was the heat that was making Keechie feel this way; that and the change of climate. The thing they had better do was go to town and duck in and see a doctor. Keechie said no, she had just been smoking too many cigarettes and everything would be all right in a day or so.

A little before noon, Keechie said sherbert appealed to her, pints and pints of it, orange or pine-apple. Bowie said he would walk to the Drug Store and get it because it might take the delivery boy an hour to get here and he wanted her to have it while she was hungry.

263

On the newspaper rack in front of the Drug Store, there was a Noon Edition and Bowie picked it up and went on in. The Soda Clerk was at the table of two women and Bowie went on to the fountain, spread the newspaper and began to read the headlines.

Soda Clerk placed his hands, palms down, on the surface at the edge of the spread newspaper and Bowie looked up. "Dollar's worth of orange and pineapple sherbert," he said.

In this headline, the words *Prison Farm* swelled and Bowie began reading underneath it:

BINGHAM, Texas, May 29—Deputy Sheriff Oscar Dunning of Winkford County arrived here yesterday afternoon after a 650-mile trip with a bench warrant for the custody of Amos Ackerman, inmate of the Bingham Prison Farm, near here, but he was a half-hour too late to get his man alive. Ackerman, serving five years for assault with intent to kill, was shot to death by prison guards at 2:30 o'clock yesterday afternoon when he made a bold dash for freedom.

Deputy Dunning was planning on returning Ackerman to Winkford County to testify in a scheduled murder trial there.

Ackerman, a trusty and member of a chopping-cotton squad working two miles from the prison buildings, was sent back to get some tools and on the way made his ill-fated break. When he did not show up, a search was instituted and prison dogs led guards to a pile of brush just off the farm property. Ignoring the commands to halt, he was slain, prison officials stated.

The effort of Ackerman to escape, farm officials declared, was a lone attempt and not participated in by any other inmates. Extra precautions to prevent escapes were ordered by Farm Captain Fred Stammers today. There are several desperate criminals on the Farm now, including Elmo (Three-Toed) Mobley, bank robber, who arrived here last week from the State Penitentiary.

Outside, the sun stung Bowie's face like a shaving lotion and his knee-bones felt like dry sponges. He walked rapidly.

Water was gushing in the bathroom and Bowie went in there. In the filling tub, Keechie sat, her hair in a knot, water lapping the under-swell of her breasts.

"Feeling better, honey?" Bowie said.

"I'll say," Keechie said. There was the clean smell of soap and Keechie's body. Her long eye-lashes clung to the wet skin. "What have you there in your hand?" she said.

"Paper."

The lathering soap in the washrag slowed. "What's the matter?"

"Nothing. Except they got him on a goddamned farm."

"Chicamaw?"

"Yes."

Keechie turned and looked at the gushing tap and then she bent and twisted it shut.

"You can't imagine what it is to be on one of those farms," Bowie said. "He won't last six months. They don't send you out to them farms unless they want to get rid of you. If you're any kind of a man you won't last, and by God, he's a man."

Keechie placed the soap and cloth on the rack and then pulled the stopper. The draining water began to swish and gurgle.

Bowie took the bath-mat off the basin and straightened it on the tile at the side of the tub. "It's cotton-chopping time now and you know what they do to them boys? Run 'em out there like horses and kick 'em with spurs and hit 'em with saps. They drop dead out in them fields, Keechie. Five of them in one day. It was in the papers."

"Well, you can't do anything about it."

Bowie helped her over the tub's rim, put the towel about her shoulders.

"Something could be done about it all right!" he said.

"For instance?"

"I mean if a man wanted to. I could go down there with one man to drive a car and take a machine gun and clean out that whole goddamned farm. Them dirty Laws and newspapers. Calling me a Number One this and a Number One that. I could set them sonsofbitches a real pace. If I wanted to hurt somebody, I wouldn't be sittin' here twiddling my thumbs."

Keechie spread the house dress about her waist and thighs. "You call this twiddling your thumbs?"

"Aw, honey, I don't mean you and me. I do tell you, though, one thing about you and me. We got to start getting out of this place here more. Get out and enjoy ourselves for a change. Go down to some of these night clubs in that French Quarter that we're all the time hearing over the radio and do a little drinking and have a good time."

"I think we can go out a little," Keechie said.

"That's what makes you feel bad in the mornings," Bowie said. "Staying cooped up like this all the time. It's not good for anybody."

"I think we can start going out some, but I don't see any use of drinking."

"We can drink beer."

"Beer, I guess, will be all right."

"You have to drink in those places. You couldn't go in one of those places and just sit there. You'd look like a I-don't-know-what."

"I'm going to get my feet dirty if you don't go in there and get my bedroom slippers," Keechie said. "In the bottom left-hand drawer."

Bowie came back with the slippers. They were red felt with black fur. "I just happened to think. I went out of that Drug Store without paying for that newspaper. I just paid for the sherbert. I'll bet them people over there think I tried to beat them out of it."

.   .   .   .   .

Bowie waited in their paralleled parked car under the shade of the French-balconied Second-Hand Store on Chartres Street. Keechie was up yonder in that big Department Store on Canal getting a dinner gown and sandals and a wrap. They were going to do this stepping out tonight in the right way.

Bowie turned now and looked at the wrapped

boxes on the back seat. There was a white linen suit in the long box and a panama hat in the round one; white oxfords and baby-blue socks in the other. He was going to look like something himself tonight. He had a blue shirt and yellow tie like the combination Chicamaw had had.

The street on which he waited was the narrowest, craziest one he had ever seen. There were old chairs and stands and vases in front of the Antique Shop that didn't look worth ten cents a dozen and the window yonder was a crazy-quilt of oil paintings. On the corner was a bar: *Vieux Carre Haven*. A man stumbled out of the swinging doors and stood there, swaying uncertainly. He had on a white cotton shirt and faded blue-denim trousers.

If she stays much longer, Bowie thought, I'm going to duck in that bar and get a beer. It takes a woman a lot longer to do things than a man. But he had fooled around and let that girl get down to where she didn't have a thing to wear. She might as well have had a shoe clerk or a flatfoot Law for a man. Not a fellow that had got himself almost thirty thousand dollars over in Texas in a couple of months.

The drunk was coming toward Bowie's car. His

shirt was grass-stained and a tattoo showed through the torn sleeve. He grinned loosely: "You got a dime, Mack, for an old boy that sure needs a drink?"

"I'll give you a quarter to get that stinking breath out of my face," Bowie said. He put a half-dollar in the cupped hand. "I just got out Stir this morning," Stink Breath said. "Thirty days I done."

"I don't give a damn," Bowie said. "Get on."

Stink Breath moved toward the bar, his hands spread like an exhausted wrestler, disappeared inside. Toward the waterfront, the whistle of a tugboat groaned.

Why couldn't a man get hold of some thief lawyer, Bowie thought, and get him to write out a Bench Warrant? Then get a Sheriff's badge and a big hat. He could go on one of them prison farms, show that and take any man off he wanted to. Them Farm Captains and Bosses couldn't see nothing but that Warrant.

A man in a beret and golf knickers stopped now in front of the window of oil paintings, shaded his forehead and pressed against the glass. He scratched his thigh.

It could be done all right, Bowie thought. Just go on that Farm like you owned it and flash your badge and be from one of those far western counties out by El Paso. Deputies and sheriffs were going on them farms everyday and gettin' men.

Keechie was coming, stepping around other pedestrians, headed for the car. Bowie pushed out the door. "I begin to think you had fell in somewhere," he said.

"They are going to get the things out by five o'clock," Keechie said. "Sure good to be back here. All those women crowding around give me the creeps."

"Lady, could you spare a dime to a man that hasn't had a bite to eat?" It was Stink Breath, his face framed in the lowered window of the car.

"Get to hell away from here," Bowie said.

"Lady, if you can't spare anything but a nickel."

Bowie pushed the door on his side out with his foot. "Bowie," Keechie called. "Bowie!"

Bowie grasped Stink Breath's collar, kicked him in the seat. The collar ripped in his hands. He kicked again. "If you don't want to get your head stomped in this sidewalk, you get up this street, you bastard."

Stink Breath loped up the sidewalk. The man in the beret, the two men that stood now in the Second-

Hand Store doorway, were laughing. Bowie grinned. "Bowie, get in here," Keechie said.

Bowie got in the car. "Something ought to be done about stew bums like that," he said.

"You ought to quit making a fool out of yourself," Keechie said.

They moved from the curb. "I'll bet he takes his next drink standing up," Bowie said.

Fastened couples churned to the beating music in a center of foaming light, but here among the tables and under the low ceiling, Bowie and Keechie sat in lavender darkness. The Mexican musicians on the palm-screened platform were playing *La Paloma*. Bowie beat on the gray tablecloth with his index finger. Now Keechie pressed a cigarette in the clay ashtray that was shaped like a sombrero. "You sure like Spanish music, don't you?" she said.

"That's one thing them Chilis can do."

"I like it too."

"I don't see anything to that dancing out there though, do you?"

"I never did care about dancing."

Bowie touched the frosted glass of beer. "Looks silly to me. Switching your tail around. Look at that gink out there, that four-eyed one, the one with the girl in the blue dress? . . . Don't he think he's a card now?"

Keechie lifted her glass, took a sip of the foamless beer and put it down. "You didn't think that when that Mexican girl was dancing," she said.

"What did I do?"

"You couldn't even find time to light my cigarette."

"I don't remember that. I'm talking about that kind of dancing out there now, honey."

The waiter came and picked up Bowie's emptied glass. His shirt front was a slick gray and the knuckles of his hand looked like a row of English walnuts. "Beer?" he said.

Bowie looked at Keechie. "Want to try something a little stronger? Whisky?"

Keechie shook her head.

"Two more beers," Bowie said. The knuckles moved away.

The orchestra was playing *La Cucaracha* now and the legs of the dancing couples were working faster and more heavily. Bowie beat on the beer glass with the ashtray. "You know, Keechie, I sure wouldn't mind going down to that country. Plenty of fellows have gone done there and liked it swell and you couldn't drag them back to this country."

"I don't know whether I would like living among a bunch of foreigners or not," Keechie said.

"I tell you a man that knows the ropes of that country. That Judge Hawkins. What that man doesn't know about that country isn't on the books."

"That man."

"I've heard you could live down there for a little of nothing. You and me could live like a couple of I-don't-know-whats down there on what we got salted away. In two or three years I'll bet I could get lined up with one of those big mining companies and where would we be then? I don't know but what that is a doggone good idea, Keechie?"

Keechie put her fingers around the glass, but did not pick it up. "It might be all right."

"Now I tell you an old boy that really knows it. Chicamaw. If he was here with us I'd be ready to start out tonight. Put that boy in the back seat of our car with a .30-30 and that Mexican army couldn't stop us from crossing that border. But if anybody knows the ropes, you can make it as easy as falling off a log."

Keechie got up and pulled her wrap off the back of the chair. "Let's go home," she said.

Bowie looked up at her. "Goodness me, honey. Why, I didn't think we was gettin' started good."

"I've had enough of this," Keechie said.

The music stopped. Bowie rose slowly. "Are you feeling bad again?"

"Yes," Keechie said.

Chairs scraped around them as the returning dancers started seating themselves. Bowie beckoned Knuckles.

Chapter XXIV

Bowie picked up another ink-crusted pen off the
table of crumbling blotters and tried the point. This
one would write. A revolving door down the dark-
ening corridor of the Post Office made a swishing,
jolting sound and Bowie watched. It was a Negro
in a porter's uniform, a bundle of papers and letters
in his arms. The Negro's shoes crackled on the tile
and echoed hollowly in the empty building. Bowie
wrote:

Dear Mr. Hawkins:
  Enclosed here is $200. I want you to get hold for me
a Bench Warrant and get a seal and everything on it.
Make it out for Elmo T. Mobley on the Bingham
Prison Farm. Make it from Becas County and fix it up
real proper and everything. Also I want a Sheriff badge.

A door swished again. The man in the straw hat
and seersucker suit dropped the letter in the slot and
presently the door bumped and Bowie was alone
again.

  I want you to please have these things ready and I
may come in on you any time. So have them ready.

Do it as soon as possible.   Remember Xmas night.   I am the same fellow.

Yours very truly,

Xmas Nite.

P. S.   *There will be another hundred for you when the goods are delivered.   X. N.*

Bowie sealed the envelope, pounded the flap with his closed hand and went over and dropped the letter in the slot.

On the sidewalk outside, he stopped and looked at the fresh, gold-painted lettering on the door of his car:

SUNSHINE CO. PRODUCTS
F. T. HAVILAND, AGENT

Around Lee Circle and then out St. Charles Avenue, Bowie drove.   Chances are I never will see that Judge, he thought, but that letter will be just in case. I thought of it and I would just keep thinking about it if I didn't get the thing off my chest.   This is just kind of like insurance, just looking ahead.

There was somebody in his apartment and Bowie brought his hand back from the knob and listened. Feet approached the door and then it opened.   It was Mrs. Lufkin.   Smelling of liquor and perfume. "Oh, how do you do, Mister Haviland?"

"All right." Through the doorway he saw Keechie sitting on the couch. She looked all right.

"Pretty warm weather we are having?" Mrs. Lufkin said.

"Too warm," Bowie said. He squeezed past Mrs. Lufkin and went inside.

"Well, goodbye," Mrs. Lufkin said.

"Goodbye," Keechie said.

Bowie closed the door. "What was that old souse doing in here?"

Keechie got up. "She wants us to move."

"Why?"

"It's nothing. She has a chance to rent it to some professor that wants it for a year and she said she knew we weren't permanent."

"You don't think she's smelled something?"

Keechie shook her head. "Oh, no."

"Well, what are we going to do?"

"There isn't anything to do, unless you want to pay her a lot of rent."

"I'll be damned if I do that. I'm ready to get out of this hot dump anyway. I can't see why anybody else would want it."

"There's plenty of places here."

"Sure. It don't worry me."

Keechie lowered herself back to the divan and lay down. "Did you get the sign on the car?"

"You ought to see it, honey. I got that fellow to do it that we saw that afternoon hanging around that Square, the one with the Jesus Christ beard. On both sides. We ought to have thought of that a long time ago."

"I thought you were never coming back."

He went over and sat down on the divan and jiggled the toe of her shoe. "It took him a pretty good while."

"Anything happen?"

"Not a thing."

After the supper of canned soup and crackers, Bowie and Keechie looked at road maps. This one here covered the whole United States and the regions were illustrated with bright-colored sketches: cattle in Texas, oil-wells in Oklahoma, shocks of wheat in Kansas.

"Doggoned if I know where to go," Bowie said. "Looks like it would be easy with all this to pick from."

"Well, we don't have to leave New Orleans, you know."

"Oh, I'm fed up on this town, honey. It's just too doggone hot."

Keechie pointed at the Southwest Texas region. "Right in there somewhere is the place we lived."

"That's another place you couldn't drag me," Bowie said.

"Or any place else in Texas," Keechie said.

Bowie tapped the Gulf of Mexico. "You ever seen the ocean, Keechie?"

She shook her head.

"Me neither. I'm almost thirty years old and you know I never have seen the ocean. Can you beat that? Say, how would you like to live on the ocean?"

"Sounds pretty good to me."

Bowie folded the map. "We got plenty of time. It never pays to decide a thing too quick. We got a couple of weeks and by then we'll know exactly where we want to light out for."

"Sure," Keechie said.

.　　.　　.　　.　　.

Keechie whimpered in her sleep again and this time Bowie sat up and looked at her. In the moonlight that filtered through the crêpe myrtle and screen, he saw her mouth pucker like a child and she whimpered again. A mosquito sang with needle-like vibration in Bowie's ear and he waved his hand over Keechie's head. She was quiet now and he eased back, moving his hand over her head from time to time.

It's malaria, he thought. That's what it is. These goddamned mosquitoes.

Keechie sobbed out. It was a dry, throat-lodging cry. She turned over, her face toward the window and lay quiet. The mosquito sang, and he raised up and fanned furiously.

Back in the kitchen, the clock ticked, smothered now by the rush of a speeding car on the avenue; ticked again. She had bought that clock in Antelope Center and of all things to bring. She bought it the same day she got that big gunny sack of Irish potatoes. They had left it and there wasn't a fourth of them used.

Keechie made sounds now like she was losing her breath and he placed his hand on her shoulder and shook gently: "Keechie, Keechie. What's the matter, honey?"

She raised, her eyes wide open. "What is it?" she said. "Bowie?"

"You ain't feeling well, honey."

"What is it?"

"Are you hurtin'? Hurtin' any place, honey?"

Keechie let her head back on the pillow. "I'm all right."

"You must have been dreaming. Nightmare or something."

She did not say anything. An automobile horn sounded on the avenue, a street-car was coming.

"You been crying in your sleep, Keechie."

"I had a dream. I guess that was it."

"What was it?"

"Forget it. I'm all right."

The street-car grated in a stop in front of the house; ground and clicked on.

'Did you think you were falling off something? I've dreamed that. Gun breaking in my hand. I dreamed I couldn't make my Dad hear me a hundred times."

"I dreamed you had gone away," Keechie said.

"Me?"

"It's all right now. Go on and go to sleep. You're going to be worn out in the morning."

"Where did I go?"

"I don't know. You had just gone and I thought I was trying to find you. I couldn't find you."

"Well, there's no danger of me going any place without you."

"You went to town yesterday."

"That's different. I mean off any place. No, honey, it looks like you and me are going up the same road together."

"Up the same road?"

"It sure looks that way."

"Is that the way you want it, Bowie?"

"That's the way I want it, honey, but sometimes I think about you."

"That's the way I want it, Bowie, and you remember it."

Bowie slapped his hands together. "That damned mosquito been bothering you?"

"I hadn't noticed it," Keechie said.

"You sleepy?"

"No, I'm wide awake now."

This street-car rumbled on past and soon was a distant, fading hum.

"I been trying to figure out some place for us to go," Bowie said. "It's got me worried."

"There's plenty of places."

"You know, I have just about decided that we got to make Mexico. If only I knew the ins and outs of

284

that damned country. I could kick myself for not pumping some fellows that had been down there. But there's nothing to this, Keechie. I'm not going to really feel good about us until we're plumb out of this country."

"We can go to Mexico."

"If I just knew the ropes about all that border down there and just knew one of them Thief officials down there that Chicamaw was telling me about. Now you take old Hawkins. I don't know but what it would be a good idea to go and see him."

"Not him," Keechie said.

"Why not?"

"There's plenty of other men that know about Mexico."

"Who?"

"I don't know, but there's plenty."

"But who?"

"There's plenty of men that know."

"But who, Keechie? That don't do no good. Just name me somebody that we could go to and he would give us all the lowdown that we got to have? I'm not any plain tourist, you know. I'm not the governor of this state, you know."

"Now don't get smart. What I am telling you is

that you don't have any business back there in Texas. Or around anybody that knows you."

Bowie clutched at the air. "I'm going to get up and brain this mosquito in just about two seconds."

There was a little wind and stirred leaves of the crêpe myrtle sighed on the screen.

"Do you really want to go to Mexico, Bowie?"

"It's about all I know to do."

"Do you think Hawkins can really help?"

"I don't know of anybody else. I was just as sure you would take me up when I mentioned him about that. I even dropped him a line."

"When?"

"When I was getting that sign put on. That day."

"Yesterday, you mean?"

"Yes."

"Why didn't you tell me?"

"I just didn't. I'm telling you now."

"Did you write about Chicamaw?"

"Yes."

Keechie sat up.

"Now look here, Keechie. Now don't start that. Honey, I'm just worried to death." He sat up.

Keechie got off the bed. "You needn't say any more. That's all I want to know."

"Now look here, Keechie. Where you going?"

"What difference does that make?"

"Now look here, Keechie. Now come on, honey."

"Which is it, Bowie? Make up your mind right now. Once and forever. Which is it, Chicamaw or me?"

"It's you. If it wasn't you, I'd been down on that farm long before now and cleaning it from one end to the other gettin' him off. I know now how you feel about it, Keechie. I'm just learning. You been a Little Soldier to me and I'm going to play square with you."

Keechie shivered.

"As long, honey, as I'm any good to you, I'm going to stay with you. I'm telling you straight now, Keechie. I've had things on my mind and I don't mind admitting it to you, but they're all over. That's it, Keechie. The best I know how to tell you."

Keechie lowered herself to the edge of the bed. "Did you really want to see that lawyer about Mexico?"

"When we were talking while ago? . . . Yes, I did. I meant it."

Keechie picked up the edge of the twisted sheet and shook it with a flapping sound out over Bowie.

Then she folded it back on her side of the bed and got under it.

"And you think the lawyer is the only one to see?" Keechie said.

"I leave it up to you, Keechie. It's all up to you."

"When do you want to go?"

"I leave that up to you."

"Tomorrow?"

"It suits me."

The clock was ticking again now in the kitchen. A truck passed on the narrow street by their window and presently there was the sound of milk bottles clattering in a tin rack. The moonlight was gone now and the sleeping-room was dark. Bowie raised up and listened to Keechie's even breathing. She was sleeping sound. He eased back, lay there a moment and then cautiously pulled up his foot and scratched the mosquito bite again.

Chapter XXV

THE moon had an eye-squinching brightness, radiating six splintered beams, broad as planks. It deepened the dark hollows of Keechie's eyes, shadowed the lines that slashed her face from cheek bones to tight lips. She sat there in their car, parked on the by-road just off the highway, her eyes closed, head resting on the back of the seat.

Bowie, standing on the ground with one foot on the running board, looked again toward the lights of MacMasters, as golden as oil lamps in the clear air. They had stopped here a little after sundown, deciding it was best to wait until ten o'clock or so and be sure that Hawkins would be at home.

"You feel any better, honey?" Bowie said.

"I want something ice-cold to drink," Keechie said. "I know I would feel a lot better if I had a cold soda pop."

"We'll get it when we gas up. The very first thing. I wish now we had stopped back up the road, but there was just so many Square Johns hanging around then."

"I can get along without it."

Bowie moved around the front of the car, got under the wheel. "We can go now," he said. "To hell with this waiting."

The neon sign on the left, at the city's edge, read: *Alamo Plaza Courts*. It burned in front of a filling station and behind that was a court of white frame cottages. On a bench under the shed of the station sat a man, an old fellow, licking a cone of ice cream. Bowie turned in and the old man rose.

"Fill it up," Bowie said. He went on to the big wooden ice-box.

The spring of the screen door whined and Bowie looked up. The woman coming out was Mattie. She was heavier; gold on her teeth. "Hi you do," she said.

"Okeh," Bowie said. He brought a bottle out of the icy water.

"Passing through?" Mattie said.

Bowie moved his head, indicating the old man holding the hose by the clicking pump.

"Papa," Mattie said.

"Just passing through," Bowie said.

Mattie looked at Keechie in the car, and Bowie jerked the bottle's cap and started back.

"Who is that?" Keechie said.

"T-Dub's sister-in-law." She took the bottle from his hand. "It's cold. She's Real People."

"I'll drink this when we get started."

"Go ahead and drink it, honey. I'll get plenty to carry."

Mattie lifted the ice-box top for Bowie. "How is everything around here?" he said.

"Okeh," Mattie said.

"How's the husband?"

"Still In There."

Bowie ran his hands over the bottles. "That's too bad."

"The cokes are at that end if that's what you are looking for," Mattie said.

"How's my heat around here?" Bowie said.

"You can find better places to run around in."

Papa hung the hose on the rack. "How's your oil?" he said. His voice squeaked like the broken note of a clarinet. "All right," Bowie said. He paid Mattie.

"Take care of yourself," Mattie said.

"Same to you," Bowie said.

The air on the boulevard was cool and clean. Out at its end was Hawkins' house.

"Aren't you going to drink that, honey?" Bowie said.

"Not now."

"What's the matter?"

"I'm afraid it might come up."

"Doggone, sugar."

"I think I had better lie down in the back. If I lie down a little while I think I will feel better."

Bowie drew alongside the curbing, stopped, got out and helped Keechie into the back. He took her coat, spread it over her feet, got back under the wheel and drove on.

There were four unoccupied automobiles parked in front of Hawkins' house. The church was dark.

"What are those cars, Bowie?" Keechie said.

"You just lay back down now, honey."

"I feel better. You think it's all right to go up there?"

"I'll be right back now before you can turn around. You just take it easy now."

The porch planks creaked and gave under Bowie's steps and then he knocked on the door. Under the half-raised blind he could see the trousered legs of men seated at a card table.

The door parted and there was a middle-aged woman in a black dress and white-lace collar.

"Judge in?"

"Why, yes. Won't you come in?"

"I'll just wait here."

The woman hesitated. "Who can I tell him?"

"Mister Knight. Mister Knight."

Bowie watched the legs through the window. The card table moved and then feet were coming to the door.

The porch globe showered light. Hawkins was in shirt sleeves and had a pipe in his right hand. He switched it quickly, reached and then the porch was dark again. "Wait a minute," he said. The door closed and Bowie backed down off the porch steps, his fingers grasping the butt of the gun under his arm.

The door opened again and Bowie went back up on the porch and took the extended envelope. It was heavy and he felt the badge's pin. "You busy?" he said.

Hawkins nodded toward the window. "Company," he whispered.

"I want to get some low down on Mexico."

Hawkins shook his head. "Can't help you there, son. That's the Sheriff in there."

"Okeh," Bowie said.

His heels clicked on the sidewalk toward the car. I promised him another hundred, but to hell with him. He's just a little too busy. I don't need this damned stuff anyway. *Where's Keechie?*

She lay face down in the bottom of the car, her left arm crooked like it was broken. "Keechie," he said. "Keechie." She was limp and heavy. "Keechie, honey. Baby. Keechie." Her teeth were clenched and he couldn't hear her breathing. He straightend her on the seat, got up in front and his hand shook on the knob above the grinding gears.

Papa pushed off the bench and approached. "Where's a vacant cabin?" Bowie said.

"Just about what kind of a price do you have in mind, Mister?"

"Any of 'em."

"We got some for a dollar and a half and some for . . ."

"Where's that woman that was around here?"

"You mean my darter? The girl that was . . ."

"Where is she?" Bowie started getting out of the car.

The screen's spring rasped and then Mattie came. "I got to have a place," Bowie said.

Mattie went around into the Court and Bowie followed her in the car. At the far, low end she pointed at the corner cabin and Bowie parked in front of it. Mattie went on in and turned on the light.

Bowie lowered Keechie to the bed, straightened the skirt down over her knees. Her face was drained, the lines deep. Mattie stood in the half-opened screen.

"I can't figure it out," Bowie said. He picked up a towel off the foot of the bed and went to the sink and turned on the water. "I can't figure it out. Go get a doctor, Mattie. Go on and get a doctor out here."

He started bathing Keechie's face. "Go on, Mattie. For Christ's sake." Mattie left.

He held the sopping towel under the running water again, went back and rubbed the back of her neck, pressed it under her collar on her chest. "Come on, Little Soldier. Show your old man you

got it in you. You bet you got it in you. You bet
you have . . ."

Her body quivered and then she sucked in with
parted lips. "That's a girl. That's a girl." Her
eyes opened and she moved her head from side to
side and then suddenly looked at him. "Did you
see him?" she said.

"Everything's swell, kiddo. Don't you worry
about it one minute. Everything's swell."

"I'm glad." Her mouth twisted and she reached
and clutched Bowie's hand. "Something is wrong
with me, Bowie. I hate to tell you. I know it."

"Don't worry, honey. The doctor is coming.
Don't you worry."

Keechie closed her eyes and Bowie took the dry
towel and wiped her face. Then he took off her
shoes. "I'm glad," she said. It was toneless, like she
was talking in her sleep.

Bowie sat on the stone edge of the fish pond in the
Court's center, watching the Doctor, a little man in
a tan suit, through the half-raised blind of the cabin.
I ought to have stayed in there. That Doctor's got
sick people on his mind and not criminals. That
Mattie.

The lights of a car brightened the yard. Papa

came around and the car followed him, an old machine with packed running boards. It went on around to the row on the other side.

"I just can't get over it," Bowie said out loud.

The door of the cabin opened, laying a slab of light on the grass, and then Mattie was coming out. Bowie went to her. "What does he say?" he said.

"There's nothing wrong with her except she's pregnant," Mattie said. "I could have told you that."

"Who said it?"

"He did. Anybody could tell."

Bowie looked at the light from the half-raised blind. "I don't want to get mixed up any farther in this," Mattie said. "You're going to have to go on." Bowie did not answer. He moved toward the cabin; into the smell of licorice and paregoric.

The Doctor had a splotch of moustache over his mouth and sagging eyerims. "That is the only thing to do," he said. "Just keep her quiet and lying on her back and I think she will come out of it fine. But she cannot keep this up. I have given her something and that is going to keep her asleep quite a while. Rest is the thing."

Keechie's breasts were rising and falling in even

breathing. "She sure is sleeping like she is awfully tired," Bowie said.

"That is the best thing," Doctor said. "Now I have put some medicine there on the table there and tomorrow, if she is still in pain, you can give it to her. She is likely to sleep a good while, and if she does awaken she more than likely will go right back to sleep again."

"She sure is sleeping."

"If you need me, call me," Doctor said.

"Sure, Doctor. Don't worry about that."

Bowie sat now on the chair by the sink in the cabin's darkness, watching Keechie's form, listening to her breathing. He got up now and touched her straightened arm, picked it up and put it on her breast; placed it back by her side. Then he left the cabin.

Mattie came out and walked around with him into the deep shadow of the station's side. "That girl can't be moved," Bowie said.

"I don't want anything happening around here," Mattie said. "I've done all I'm going to in this."

"If it's money that's holding you, don't worry about that."

"I don't want any of your money. All I want you

to do is get off this place." The screen sounded and Mattie turned her head and started off.

"Hold it," Bowie said. Mattie stopped. "Now you listen to me," Bowie said. "You're a thief just like me and you ain't going to yellow on me when I'm asking you to lay off. She's not going to be moved, see, and if you or anybody else don't like it, it's just too goddamned bad."

Mattie walked on away.

Keechie had not moved. He lifted the blind, a square of moonlight baring her feet. He pulled the blind back down, took off her hose and placed the sheet over her legs.

The Court was quiet. In Bowie's ears, the cricket-ringing sounds were growing. That yellow Hawkins, he thought. The two-faced sonofabitch.

If only that Indian was here. Them white teeth. Little Soldier, it can't be got around. They got me in a rank now. The whole, lousy, yellow bunch.

Water dripped in the sink and he got up and tightened the tap.

We got to hole-up right pretty soon, girl. There ain't no *ifs* and *ands* about it. I have fooled around long enough.

You got Something Else to think about now, Little

Soldier. Old Bowie is not so big in this picture now. But they can't put nothing on you, Keechie. They just can't do it. Don't you let them make you think it for a minute. Don't you let 'em.

The dropped match from his fingers rattled on the floor and he watched her. She did not move and he breathed again. But you're plumb out, honey. You're not going to be waking up until away in tomorrow.

If that Chicamaw was here, Keechie, we could beat them easy. He's the only friend we got in this world. You don't know it, Keechie, but I do, honey. He's the only one in this world that would help us. You and me are going up this road together and we got to find us a Hole and pull it in after us. 'Specially now. You can't run these roads much longer. That Mexico, Keechie. They ain't but one person in this world that can get us down there. Just one.

Somewhere in the night a dog bayed.

Say it worked, Keechie. Say I run that hundred and twenty miles over to that Farm from here, get there by seven o'clock this morning and spring that boy? You would be asleep, honey, and never know a thing about it. I would be back and you'd wake up and that Chicamaw would be with us and then

I'd like to see somebody stop us. Honey, we'd be holed up in Mexico two days from now. Deep, Keechie. Pulled in after us.

The dog bayed again.

Well, say it didn't work, Keechie? Say it flopped? All right, Little Soldier, you got Somebody Else to think about now. Old Bowie stepped out don't mean so much. You don't have nobody to beat, Keechie. They can't hang a thing in this world on you. All you have ever done is just kind of run around with me. Say it flopped all right, Keechie? Well, there you are.

Bowie got up and buttoned his coat.

The high, net-wire fence was broken here by a wooden Arch: *Bingham Prison Camp*—and Bowie left the highway and turned his machine through it. Stone-bordered beds of flowers colored the sides of the gray road that led up there to the Buildings. There was the smell of sweet-peas.

There was the Office, a squat, brick building with an empty flagpole and behind it, long, barrack-looking buildings, stone foundations whitewashed, and barns.

A figure in the white sacking of a convict, on his

knees and breaking clods around the rose bush with his hands, looked up as Bowie got out of his car. He lowered his head as Bowie passed on toward the Office porch, the two men in khaki uniforms sitting on a bench, cartridge belts around their waists, shotguns beside them.

"How do you do?" Bowie said.

The heads of the Guards moved. "Howdy . . . Hidy."

Bowie indicated the porch-shadowed door. "Captain Stammers in?"

The two nodded.

Bowie entered the smell of disinfectant, looked at the face framed in the top of the high, bookkeeper's desk, a Convict's; moved down the desk's length and stopped before the two men on the bench. The big one was dressed like the men on the porch, the other in blue serge trousers and white shirt. He got up.

"Captain Stammers?" Bowie said.

"That's me," the man said. He had thin black hair, parted in the middle, and held his left arm crooked as if it were in pain. He did not have a gun on. Bowie extended his hand. "I'm Sheriff Haviland, Becos County."

Captain Stammers pumped Bowie's hand. "Glad to know you, Sheriff. What can I do for you?"

The Guard on the bench got up and moved toward the door. "See you after while, Captain," he said.

"I want to see a boy you got on your place here," Bowie said. "Elmo Mobley."

"Yeah, we got him. Let me see now. He's in Boss Hebert's squad today I think. Now what is it we can do for you there?"

"I have a Bench Warrant, but I don't intend to take him." Bowie pulled the paper from his inside coat pocket and handed it to Stammers. "I just wanted to talk to him a little on this trip." The paper crackled as Stammers opened the Warrant:

THE STATE OF TEXAS

To the Honorable *Sheriff A. T. Haviland, Sheriff of Becos County,* Texas, GREETING;

On this *12 day of May A.D.* 1935, it appearing to the Court that there is now pending on the docket of this Court, a certain case entitled the STATE of Texas VS. *Elmo T. Mobley,* being our case *No. 754,* wherein said defendant is charged with the offense of murder,

Whereas, said case . . .

"You don't want to take him?" Stammers said. He started folding the paper.

"No, I just want to talk to him."

Stammers went over and picked the gray hat off the hook and turned and touched his left arm. "Neuritis, bad," he said.

"I've heard that it's bad," Bowie said.

On the porch, Stammers said to the three guards: "Watch that telephone, boys."

Bowie moved toward his car and Stammers followed. "We can just go in my car," Bowie said.

"Did you ever hear of anybody that found out anything to help it?" Stammers said.

"It just has to wear off, I hear," Bowie said.

Stammers pointed at the dirt road that twisted back of the building and toward the cotton-fields. Bowie moved onto it.

The cotton was fresh and green, the earth around it freshly hoed. "Mighty nice stand you got out here, Captain."

"Rain last week," Stammers said. He picked up his left hand and placed the elbow on his stomach. "Nice rain last week."

Puffs of dust rose from the chopping hoes of the working convicts yonder, fifteen or twenty men; two men on horses, shotguns in the cradles of their arms, watching. Faces of working men lifted and looked at the car, bent back again.

The horseman with the boots and jagged Spanish spurs approached. He was a heavy man with a billowing waist. There was a pistol on his belt; a rifle in the saddle scabbard.

"Mobley is in that bunch, isn't he?" Stammers said.

Spanish Spurs nodded. "Yessir."

"Bring him over here."

At the head of the squad, a figure raised, listened and then stepped out. He was coming now, the hoe in hand. Spanish Spurs spoke and Chicamaw threw the hoe down.

Chicamaw looked hard and well. He studied Bowie and then Stammers and then Bowie again.

"Get in this car, Mobley," Bowie said. "I want to talk to you a little while, boy. We'll go back up to your office, Captain."

"Sure."

Chicamaw sat in the front alongside Bowie; Stammers in the back. They were going now back up the road toward the Buildings. "You didn't stop by State and see the Warden, did you?" Stammers said.

"No, I went to Houston a different way. I'm stopping there on my way back though."

"Well, give the Warden my regards. You didn't go to the Convention this year, did you, Sheriff?"

"No, I didn't," Bowie said.

"You know I was a Sheriff for fourteen years. I'd like to have gone to that Convention this year."

Bowie nudged Chicamaw's thigh, indicated the panel pocket. Chicamaw pulled the ivory knob, grasped the pistol and turned on Stammers. "It's a break, Captain," he said. "Sit there."

"We're going right out through this gate up here, Captain," Bowie said. "Don't you let on to nobody in no way. You understand, don't you?"

"I understand."

The porch was empty. The Convict, working around the rose bush, looked up and then stood. Bowie passed the Office and the chaff of the road began peppering the fenders. He swerved up and onto the highway; opened the throttle wide.

"Well, boys, this is going to cost me," Stammers said.

"Don't let it get you down, Cap," Chicamaw said.

"It seems to me now that I had seen you before, Sheriff, but by God, I still don't know."

"Just forget it, Captain," Bowie said. "I guess you'll find out soon enough. How long do you think it will be before your boys back there figure something is wrong?"

"I wish I knew."

Chicamaw looked deeper in the car pocket, reached in it and explored with his hand.

"What you looking for?" Bowie said.

"Nothing," Chicamaw said.

"This is going to cost me, boys," Stammers said.

"Tell that to the Warden, Cap," Chicamaw said.

"You been treated pretty good on that Farm, boy," Stammers said.

"Pipe down, Chicamaw," Bowie said. "For Christ's sake."

The highway sign read: *MacMasters . . . 68 mi.* At the off-road, Bowie turned and they drove along through the timber. After a half-mile, Bowie stopped and they all got out and crawled through the fence, and in the woods Bowie tied Stammers to a tree.

Heat glimmered from the highway's cement slabs. "Say they been pretty good to you back there?" Bowie asked.

"They don't use a bat or barrel any more," Chicamaw said. "Them big political boys stopped all that. They'd still do it, but they're afraid they'll lose them sixty-dollar jobs."

"That's something though."

Chicamaw turned and looked in the back of the car. "You're not going to tell me you didn't bring no pint along, are you?"

Bowie shook his head. "No liquor in this party, Chicamaw. I got some business that needs attending and it takes a clear head."

"I don't believe you're ever going to be human," Chicamaw said. "I tell you, man, I don't see how you do it. You get out here and run these roads and pull a thing like that back yonder and beat these Laws right and left, and, by God, Bowie, I don't see how in the hell you do it. You're just a big country boy and just chumpy as hell at times and yet you do it."

"What did you want to do, stay back yonder?"

"Me? Don't kid yourself. Not with that Texaco City trouble still up in the air. Man, I been thinking any day here they would come. You're the boy they want on that. Them fingerprints of yours sure played hell there. I was pretty foxy in that though.

They got you tagged on that, but what they got on me for sure?"

"It's raised a lot of heat all right," Bowie said. "That trouble."

"You seem to beat it all right," Chicamaw said. "You just keep going right on."

"Just luck," Bowie said.

"That's it. Call it that. You're no more a criminal than that damned radiator cap there. And yet you do it. It rips my guts out. You're just a big Sunday-school chump and yet you can pull a thing like that back yonder and run these roads and make me look like thirty cents."

Bowie's head jerked. "You going crazy? What the hell is gettin' the matter with you?"

"It rips my guts out. Take you and on top of that a damned little old girl that was never outside of a filling station and, by God, the papers don't do nothing but print about you all the time. Why, it makes me look like a damned penny slot machine . . ."

Bowie stopped at the side of the highway.

"What's the matter?" Chicamaw said. "What's this idea?"

Bowie got out of the car and walked around and

pulled out Chicamaw's door. "Come on," he said. "You sonofabitch, come on."

"Good God, Bowie. What's got into you?"

"Get out."

Chicamaw got out.

"The only reason I'm not letting you have it right here," Bowie said, "is because there might be some dogs that will do it."

"Listen, Bowie. I want to go see my folks. I ain't never seen 'em, Bowie. Let me get that gun in the car."

"Get."

Chicamaw started running up the road.

A car with a blaring loudspeaker and bannered with lettering about a picture show was the only moving machine on the heat-stilled Square of Mac-Masters. The music was *Stars and Stripes Forever*. Bowie turned off the Square and moved out the highway that led to the Courts. Nossir, God, I never asked nothing from you before. Not a thing in this world. But just let me get up there the rest of the way now. And if it ain't asking too much, keep her still asleep. Just let her wake up and I'll be sittin' there. . . .

The driveway and yard of *Alamo Plaza Courts*

were deserted. Bowie drove on down and parked parallel in front of the closed door and lowered blind.

She lay there on the bed, her eyes closed, still breathing, just as he had left her. He looked around. Nothing had been moved. Nothing. Thanks, God.

The afternoon heat pressed against the cabin, making the walls as hot as a dying stove. The roof's tar melted and smelled. Bowie stood above Kee-chie, flapping the wet towel. The little curls on her forehead trembled under the cooling air. Honey, you got to be waking up pretty soon and eating some-thing. I mean real wide awake.

Dusk seeped into the room now, drying the sweat on Bowie's forehead, stiffening the hairs on his arms. Keechie stirred greater now, and he bent over. Her eyes opened. They were like petals submerged in tiny bowls of unchanged water.

"Bowie?" she said.

"Hello, sleepyhead."

"Bowie?"

"It's about time you were waking up."

"You wouldn't leave me, would you?"

"Me? You don't mean me. I should say not. Don't be silly now waking up."

"Bowie?"

"What, Keechie?"

"I mean it."

"God knows now too, Keechie. I mean it."

Keechie closed her eyes. He touched her. "Listen, Little Soldier, you got to get something inside that stomach of yours. How about a soda pop? Ice-cold to start things off?"

Keechie's head moved up and down on the pillow.

"Now let's see." Bowie stood erect and began rubbing his hands. "Just about what kind of flavor now would the little lady crave? Strawberry?"

Keechie nodded.

Bowie moved through the gloom to the door, pulled it back. *"Don't let a move out of you,"* the Voice said. It was like the swish of a missing blade. Cat with seven lives, Bowie thought. He whipped out his gun. Steampipes burst in his ears. *Seven.* He swirled in the bell of the roaring loudspeaker on the Square: *Stars and Stripes Forever.* Cat . . . *seven.* Things were wrinkling, folding gently, like paper dolls in a puff of cigarette smoke. *Strawberry . . .*

.   .   .   .   .

MacMASTERS, Texas, June 21—The crime-blazed trail of the Southwest's phantom desperado, Bowie Bowers, and his gun-packing girl companion, Keechie Mobley, was ended here early tonight in a battle with a sharp-shooting band of Rangers and peace officers who beat their covered quarry to the draw. The escaped convict, bank robber and quick-triggered killer, and his woman aide were trapped in the cabin of a tourist camp, one mile east of this city, and killed instantly in one burst of machine and rifle fire.

Stirred to a vengeful heat after Bowers' sensational liberation of his old pal, Elmo (Three-Toed) Mobley, from the Bingham Prison Farm early this morning, grim-faced officers swooped down on the camp. After the battle, Bowers lay sprawled in the doorway of the cabin, the girl inside on the floor. A gun was clutched in Bowers' hand, another near the hand of Keechie Mobley. Both were bullet-riddled, their deaths instantaneous.

A bag containing almost $10,000 in currency was recovered in the splintered cabin, also a quantity of what officers declared was narcotics.

The killings brought to a dramatic climax a search of more than a year for the desperado and his companion. Wanted in at least four states for murders, bank robberies, filling-station holdups, kidnapings of peace officers, Bowers had become one of the Southwest's most feared criminals.

This peaceful, thriving little city was stunned tonight by the news that it had harbored in its environs this pair. Knots of excited people thronged the streets tonight and crowds were viewing the bodies in a local undertaking parlor.

Tall, steel-eyed Ranger Captain Leflett refused to comment at length on the case, declaring that the owners of the tourist camp where the pair was slain, were unaware of the identity of their notorious guests. When he reported to his Chief in the State Capital, he declared simply: "Chief, we have got them."

Elmo Mobley, freed by Bowers earlier in the day when Captain Stammers was kidnaped, was captured by a farmer who became suspicious when he saw Mobley running in the road and then recognized the prison clothing.

Rewards totaling more than $1,000 will be distributed among the twenty picked officers who took part in the slayings.

Supplied a tip before daybreak this morning, local officers began acting quickly. Telephone and telegraph wires hummed to the State Capital and Penitentiary. An airplane brought Ranger Captain Leflett and four men.

At the State Penitentiary, according to news dispatches received here, Warden Joel Howard admitted to reporters, it is said, that the tip was furnished after a "deal" had been made for the liberation of an inmate in the prison there. "Bowers was a ruthless, cunning criminal," Warden Howard declared, "and we had to exert every resource to bring him down."

THE END